Sidetracked

Transition Trilogy

Book One

John T. Peters

Also, by
John T Peters

Destroyed Trust

Africa Beckons

Author Website

http://www.johntpeters.uk

Book cover by:
Jane korunoski

Sidetracked

CHAPTER ONE

Scientists say it takes 66 days to change your life.
I believe that sometimes it only takes a second.
There are moments in our lives that can alter our
directions forever.
You will know when it happens to you.
Sometimes it starts with a smile from a stranger or a
kind word.
Sometimes it is a missed turn that diverts you to an
unexpected place.

My life-changing moment came one sunny winter morning while standing outside the post office where I worked, trying to absorb the heat that was on offer from the winter sun before the daily rush.

The post office was set about ten metres off the main road and surrounded by a tall hedge. Behind the post office were the telephone exchange and the technician's carrier room. The postboxes, made of metal built into the sidewall of the building, on its veranda, linked to the main road by a separate footpath and entrance gate.

As I enjoyed my early morning cigarette while standing near the private post boxes, the most beautiful girl I had ever seen appeared through the gate in the hedge. She seemed to glide up the path approaching the individual post boxes, dressed in snug-fitting jeans that accentuated her well-shaped hips and legs. Not being courageous and scarred of rejections, I was stunned by her beauty and left completely dumbstruck; I could only mumble, 'Good morning'.

If only I had a bit more inner strength, I would have handled this meeting more confidently.

She turned towards me and cheerfully greeted me in a soft, melodious voice. I felt as if her eyes melted me on the spot and I could only stare open-mouthed, admiring the way her curly light brown hair framed her smooth, sculpted face. Her inviting ripe lips parted, showing a set of even white teeth. I looked at her and knew as sure as the sun will rise tomorrow, that I loved her more than anything I had ever seen or imagined on earth or hoped for anywhere else.

She must have realised the effect she had on me, and her lovely, large brown eyes flickered over me; I knew that she had carefully weighed me up.

The meeting left me speechless. Having never experienced such a feeling in the presence of a girl before, I found it a bit unsettling. At that moment, I knew I had never seen anything more beautiful in my life. I felt intoxicated merely thinking about her and tingled all over with excitement, reflecting that this must be love, Or close enough to it.

I finished my cigarette in a daze, wondering from where such a beautiful girl could have appeared. I returned to my duties inside but was not able to concentrate on what I was doing. My colleagues started to correct me.

Jabulani, the mail delivery person, complained, 'Inkosi, you are putting these letters in the wrong streets. The people in town will say that Jabulani is a bad delivery boy if they get the wrong mail.'

I replied, a bit defensively, 'You have such few letters to deliver that we should not have to sort them for you in street order.'

There were only a few letters for delivery as most farmers and businesses rented private boxes, and the mail for the locals sorted in alphabetical order to be collected from Jabulani at the post office. He seemed to know everyone in town. We all suspected that he charged the residents for looking after their mail.

I remained in a state of shock for the rest of the day, cursing myself for not even checking the post box number she had opened.

Well, here I am, James Hammond, in the year 1970, a city boy with little experience of the opposite sex and only one previous girlfriend at school. Now employed by the post office in the village of Lusikisiki, I was infatuated with this lovely girl whose name and address I did not know. I was only aware I was smitten. She could have been a ghost for all I knew.

The staff at the post office was Mr Visagie, the postmaster, and me. Two African clerks Cedric and

Paul, and Jabulani, who was our mail delivery person. Two ladies operated the telephone exchange: the elderly Mrs Umpleby and a young girl called Mary, the daughter of the local magistrate. There was also a telephone technician to support us with faults and new installations; this was Alan Stern, who also stayed in the local hotel.

Being an elderly lady, Mrs Umpleby was incredibly set in her ways and lived on her own in a cottage near the post office. There was a rumour that the police feared for the life of any intruder that attempted to burgle Mrs Umpleby. It was alleged she kept a fully loaded sawn-off shotgun in bed with her.   It was common speculation in the bar as to what damage it would cause if she fired the weapon in the confined space of her bedroom. She also refused to work after 5 pm, which caused a big problem as the exchange stayed open until 11 pm. One could not expect Mary to work until 11 pm every day; she was reluctant to work after 7 pm.

People of the village were also against the girls working in the evening. Ostensibly this was for safety reasons. However, it was common knowledge that they eavesdropped on all conversations, especially when it was quiet and they were bored. It was then up to Alan and me to man the exchange in the evenings between 7 pm and 11 pm. As Alan's work was mostly on farm lines out of town, he could not be relied upon to return in time to help regularly.

The overtime was welcome for doing exceedingly little. Alan and I had an arrangement with the hotel to send our meals and whatever drinks we required to the exchange. It also gave us ample opportunity to make free telephone calls to friends and family.

The village name Lusikisiki stems from the natural sound caused by the wind blowing through the dry reeds in the marshes below the village. A chief's kraal believed to have occupied the site of the present town before the Europeans came, and even then, it was called Lusikisiki.

The white settlement had its origin in 1894. Mpondoland then annexed to the Cape Colony, when a magistrate took up residence there. In 1950, the district had 110,000 inhabitants and was subject to the Paramount Chief of Eastern Mpondoland, who had his Great Place at Qaukeni near the village. Mpondoland is now part of the Transkei, which is the homeland of the Xhosa people. About 350 whites resided in the town and on nearby farms.

Lusikisiki is a small farming village surrounded by a feast of natural wonders and waterfalls. The town itself consisted of a post office, a bank, two general stores, a liquor store, a wholesaler serving all the trading stores, a courthouse, a police station, two churches (one being the Catholic church with a convent), and, obviously, the Royal Hotel.

Single men such as me manned many of the businesses. Most of us lived in the hotel, except for the police, who had their living quarters attached to the police station. However, they also spent most of their off-duty hours in the hotel bar.

The term 'hotel' is probably an overstatement as it consisted of only a single-story white building with a red-painted corrugated iron roof, and comprised of about nine or ten bedrooms, a shared bathroom, a lounge, a dining room, and a public bar. It had a lovely wide veranda overlooking grass lawns, with tables and chairs facing the main road. Travellers on their way to Port St John's often stopped there to relax with a cup of tea and sandwiches or an ice-cold beer. Savouring the sunshine and the crisp fresh air, only spoiled by the occasional arrival of the maroon coloured government bus, polluting the surroundings with toxic diesel fumes.

Breakfast in the hotel, served at 7 am sharp, was an incredibly active and noisy scene as every person without a hangover loudly discussed the previous night's activities, such as darts and the various card games, who was cheating who, and what money was outstanding to whom.

CHAPTER TWO

After completing my education, I joined the post office, knowing that my conscription for eighteen months national service training was imminent. It was a common practice as if you work for a government department; you received full pay while undergoing your training.

Although the post office was not my career choice, it was a necessity as I needed the income during the months of national service.

Training in one of the armed forces did not inspire me with great enthusiasm and, though I was certainly no pacifist, the defence of one's country had to be for the right reasons. The very thought of being posted to an African township, being surrounded by little boys throwing stones, and having to face the choice of shooting your way to safety or being killed where you stood was unacceptable to me.

My first love was computer programming, and that was my chosen path. After my national service training, I had already a position lined up with a company in Pietermaritzburg.

After the completion of my post office training, in line with expectations, I was posted to the most remote place, where experienced staff did not volunteer or wish to go. The village was Lusikisiki on the Wild Coast of the Eastern Cape.

To me, this was a welcome change as I don't make friends easily, having a constant fear that everyone is judging me. I believe it is the result of bullying as a child. In a village of few people, there was no choice, but to be friends with everyone.

It was a particularly friendly community, and by staying at the hotel, I got to meet most residents and farmers in the bar. I got on well with all of them, but one had to be careful: like in all small towns, everyone knew each other's business. The main activities were playing darts, drinking beer, and, on weekends, exploring the magnificent countryside.

True to form, the first person I befriended was the barman called Clive. A young man of about 21 years of age, he was friendly, well built, and clean-shaven, with short, cropped hair and a friendly, warm smile. I was amazed to discover that he was awaiting a place at the Pinetown monastery to start his studies to enter the priesthood. He was extremely fond of his beer and declared that this was one of the essential duties of a good priest. The other responsibilities involved fishing, hunting, and drinking more beer. Clive's parents managed the local wholesaler and also owned a lovely cabin at the Mboyti estuary. We spent regular weekends fishing there.

Fishing at Mboyti is an experience to behold. There is no waiting for hours to get a bite; in season, the waves were a solid mass of fish, and you only had to cast in to catch one. On my first visit to Mboyti, I hooked at least thirty fish in half an hour. Crayfish were also in abundance; what's more, the young African kids netted buckets full and offered them to us fishermen for bait.

Clive also took me to see the Magwa Falls for the first time. It was a Saturday afternoon, and he and Steve, who worked in the bank and was also a resident in the hotel, were frantically searching for rope. 'Come with us, we are going to the Magwa Falls, but we need a long length of rope,' Clive remarked. Fortunately, I had some at the post office.

'Are we going to climb down the falls?' I enquired, thinking the rope was for our safety.

'Yes, certainly, it is beautiful at the bottom of the falls and a pleasant place to spend the afternoon,' Clive commented, waving me on.

The falls are only a few kilometres from town, and we were soon there preparing for the descent before I realised that the rope was for securing a case of beer to lower it safely down from ledge to ledge.

The Magwa Falls is a curtain of water that plummets 144 metres and drops into a narrow canyon formed by the past movement of the Earth's crust along a geologic fault. At only 8 km from the village, it is well worth visiting solely to see the river lurch off the precipice and down to the riverbed in the gorge below. From the clearing where one could park, you could not see the bottom as it was such a sheer drop to the bottom of the falls.

On the spine-tingling descent down, moving around a corner on one of the many ledges I spotted the footprints of a large cat, clearly defined in the moist soil and looking frighteningly fresh. "That's a leopard footprint, go carefully, we don't want to meet it cornered on one of these ledges,' Clive remarked.

I thought that it would be frightening meeting a leopard in these confined spaces. Why you would be able to count its spots, you would be that close. Being mostly nocturnal, it was unlikely, but even if one were around, it would hopefully have fled from all the noise we were making. After that, I nervously checked each ledge on our descent to the bottom of the falls.

Fortunately, we did not meet any leopards, only monkeys who were especially interested in our case of beer. Because of the monkeys' interference, the rope had to be re-tied several times to make sure it was still secure as we lowered the case downward.

On reaching the bottom of the falls, I was astounded by the magnificent sight of large boulders surrounding a beautiful pool. There was a continuous misty spray covering the whole area. This inviting scene tempted me closer, and I wanted to sit as close to the falls as possible.

Clive warned, 'Don't go near the falls, it's too dangerous. The kids throw rocks down for fun.' Right then a rock exploded with a loud crack similar to a gunshot, hitting the boulders and splintering into hundreds of pieces, like bullets ricocheting all over the place.

After some exploring and several beers, we followed the river downstream. The narrow bottom near the falls soon widened into a sizeable valley where African woman was doing their washing in the clear, slow-flowing stream of water. We did not climb back up but took the scenic route, walking from the valley below the falls back to the top where the pickup was parked.

Although on a much smaller scale, Magwa falls has been mentioned to resemble Victoria Falls in Rhodesia. The scenery was stunning; I remember gazing in a state of awe over the landscape. The proximity and the beauty of the Magwa Falls encouraged me to visit regularly.

Having a car was essential as there were no trains, only a bus depot in front of the wholesaler that also served as a petrol station. The only way in or out was by the government bus that arrived once a day, bringing the post.

All the residents of the hotel worked in town except for four German guys who were supposedly diving for some treasure on an old sunken ship called the *Grosvenor* near the mouth of the Mkweni River on the coast, about 20 km away.

The *Grosvenor* was a 729 tonne, three-masted ship belonging to the English East India Company. She was on her return voyage to England when she sank on the night of August 3, 1782, as she approached the Wild Coast, heading for a rocky spot near the mouth of the Mkweni River.

The ship believed to be carrying British gentry returning to England. The cargo alleged to contained valuables such as 2,600,000 gold pagoda coins, 1,400 gold ingots, nineteen chests of diamonds, emeralds, rubies, sapphires, and a precious jewel-encrusted gold peacock throne from India.

The value and content of the cargo are debatable. For instance, it is claimed by some that to lure salvage dealers they added the gold peacock throne. However, the shipment was of substantial value, commonly agreed by all.

The cause of the shipwreck blamed on cattle owners living along the coast, who burned the winter grasslands to stimulate summer growth. Through the sea spray and bad weather, lights in the sky were the interpretation of these fires.

Because the captain believed the *Grosvenor* to be at least 300 km from the shore, he thought that the lights in the sky were something like the Northern Lights and thus the ship continued on its course into the rugged, rocky coastline. The land was spotted slightly before dawn. Only then did the captain give the orders to turn the ship about – but it was too late. The *Grosvenor* hit an outer reef, about 400 m from the beach.

Of the 150 passengers and crew, 123 people reached the beach alive, surrounded by many of their possessions, which had floated in on the new tide.

The majority of the passengers were of good social standing, only below the nobility in position and birth, and were not used to rough conditions. Only 18 of those shipwrecked reached Cape Town, from where they got repatriated. The rest either died from rationing and privations, murdered by the Bantu or forced to live among them. A half-caste group later found in the vicinity of the wreck would seem to indicate that the white wives whose husbands died, lived with the Africans.

A century later, some gold and silver coins were found on the beach near the wreck site, leading to speculations of a vast treasure on board the *Grosvenor.* The actual wreck of the *Grosvenor* is still waiting for someone to discover and to emerge from the rocky depths with its fabled fortune.

One of the German divers was called Gunter, and he had a Minox camera that intrigued me; it was a 35mm miniature camera that could be carried in your pocket and was not readily available in South Africa. It singled him out to me, and we became friendly.

Gunter was a slim guy of medium height with curly brown hair and spoke only broken English with a heavy German accent. He related that he lived in a town called Bielefeld in Germany, and this was his first visit to South Africa. He loved diving and thought of diving for the lost treasures of the *Grosvenor* as the adventure of a lifetime.

I approved as I also loved diving, and this common interest established a bond between us. Soon we were exchanging experiences and consuming several beers as the evening passed. Gunter invited me to join them on one of his days off work as most weekends they went away.

He asked, 'James, please tell me about your diving experiences as I have to tell my friends that it is safe to take you with us.'

'I must confess that I have only dived on a few occasions using tanks. Most of my diving was with a snorkel, diving for sinkers to sell back to fishers who lost them in the first place. I did this every Sunday while attending boarding school, for pocket money,' I explained. 'Do you dive extremely deep? Unfortunately, I have not done any deep diving, and all I have done was self-taught.'

'Be assured,' Gunter replied, 'your experience sounds good enough for what we are doing. In reality, it is similar to diving for sinkers; we don't go exceptionally deep.'

Every morning the German divers set off in their old Volkswagen Kombi for the Mkweni river mouth where their camp was situated, and their diving gear was stored. It was due to whites from outside the area needing to get special permission to visit the Wild Coast as it was part of the Bantu homeland and had protected status. Even with a permit, you were not allowed more than a day visit on the coast.

Except for the towns and their immediate surrounding area, the Wild Coast fell under the jurisdiction of the Transkei. They did not see many tourists, even though the surrounding areas had magnificent natural wonders, waterfalls, and spectacular coastlines. Unbelievable fishing opportunities were available from the surf or the rocky ledges along the shore, and fly-fishing was possible in the many lagoons. During June and July, the fantastic annual sardine run takes place along the Wild Coast as whales, dolphins, sharks, gannets, and seals feast on the vast shoals of sardines that migrate along the coast.

One other off-putting factor to tourists could be the 1960 riots when a severe clash between tribesman and the police took place. Two aircraft and a helicopter dropped tear gas and smoke bombs on the crowd, and police vehicles approached from two directions. The police alleged that there were shots fired at them; they then opened fire and pursued the tribesmen who fled into the bush.

The unrest was caused by the government trying to establish tribal authorities, altering their boundaries and appointing members without the approval of the local chiefs. These riots, together with having to obtain permits to visit the area, must have contributed towards the reluctance of tourists to visit what is a paradise.

CHAPTER THREE

Lusikisiki's only claim to fame is that the millionaire medicine man Khotso Sethuntsa lived outside the town in his distinctive blue and white house, adorned with pillars, minarets, stained glass, and statues of lions.

He lived surrounded by white-robed disciples, retainers, and numerous wives and concubines. Customers from all over southern Africa and abroad flocked to him for medicines for healing, good fortune, and wealth.

He delighted in flaunting his wealth. Every year he purchased a new Cadillac at the Kokstad Agricultural Show, paid for in cash because he preferred not to use banks. He and his attendants would arrive, bearing suitcases full of banknotes, and slowly count out the money.

Khotso claimed his parents had worked for Paul Kruger, hinting that his fortune derived from the long-lost Kruger millions. Statues of Kruger and Kruger memorabilia adorned his headquarters in Lusikisiki. He predicted the winner of the Durban July horse race three times in a row. On the first occasion, he stated that Kruger had shown him the name of the winning horse in a vision.

Real fame began when he was a youthful farm worker. The farmer for whom he worked punished him, dismissing him from his employment. Shortly after that, a tornado struck the farmer's land, sweeping right through the centre of his house. Rumours spread that Khotso had brought the storm down on the farm. The conviction grew that he could work strong magic, and his business as a herbalist prospered.

He was renowned for his sorcery in the attainment of prosperity and good fortune. The most important of these magical procedures was called '*ukuthwala for wealth*', a dangerous, potent method for long-term wealth. Many who underwent "*ukuthwala*" did indeed become rich.

For this technique, spirits are summoned and only work for that specific person. The soul of '*ukuthwala*' always takes control of the life of that person, who becomes busy pleasing this spirit that he can no longer live an ordinary life because he has to carry out many sacrifices and follow many rules.

You are also entitled to many things an average person wouldn't want: a magic woman who comes to you, and you have to entertain her. In that case, you must leave your own woman or wife.

This magic woman comes in many forms, all of them frightening: it can be a goblin, snakes, or something horrific.

One of his best-selling medicines was '*ibangalala*', a herb for sexual potency. Khotso told people that he had twenty-three wives, and claimed he kept all his women sexually satisfied because he used '*ibangalala*'. Khotso claimed this powder he produced rejuvenated sexual potency. Industrial chemists at the University of Witwatersrand's Department of Botany analysed samples. The scientists were baffled by '*Ibangalala*', they were unable to prove its composition or how it worked.

He veiled himself in secrets and riddles, surrounded by controversy. Many believed he was a great healer and worker of mighty magic. Others thought his empire was an outrageous fabrication and cunning manipulation of human needs and weaknesses.

We often used to wonder why one never saw any of these foreign visitors in town or staying in the Royal Hotel. It seems that he had an office in the closest significant settlement, Kokstad, where he would meet his foreign clients. Kokstad also offered better hotel accommodation.

You could not ask too many questions from the locals as they were all scared of him, stating that he would turn them into a frog or something. We never saw him in town, but his white-robed disciples were seen frequently at the post office collecting his mail.

CHAPTER FOUR

I could not shift the image in my mind of my mysterious girl collecting her post. Her lovely brown eyes, light brown hair, perfectly sculpted face and beautiful melodious voice had utterly captivated me. Every night I would lay awake in bed thinking of her. I was obsessed with the thought of her. I found myself irresistibly attracted to her, even though I had only seen her briefly but once.

Now I stood unfailingly outside the post office each morning on the pretext of having a smoke, secretly yearning to see her again and planning what to say. And then imagining with dismay that she might not want to speak to me; after all, a girl this beautiful must be claimed already.

Maybe I should visit Khotso, the witch doctor. He could work some magic for me to influence my mysterious girl.

The days dragged on, and I plunged myself into the daily routine at work. I did not mention or ask about this girl as I did not want to sound foolish after only one hello, knowing that friends and work colleagues would laugh and poke fun at me.

After what seemed like an eternity but was, in truth, only a week, she appeared again, dressed this time in a beautiful flowing skirt that showcased her narrow waist, complemented by a white cotton blouse straining against the pressure of her ripe, round breasts.

A bit more alert than the previous meeting but still with trepidation I mumbled, 'Good morning, nice to see you again.' To my surprise, her face lit up with a warm smile, and in her soft, honeyed voice, she replied, 'Hi, what a pleasant surprise. I did not expect to see you again; I thought you were only visiting our village.'

I don't know where I got the courage from as I had this constant fear of rejection, perhaps it was her smile, but my heart skipped a beat, convinced that I had stopped breathing. I did not, for one moment, expect to receive such a warm and friendly greeting from such a lovely girl, but it gave me the confidence to put on my bravest face, smile and reply with self-assurance. 'No, I work here and live in the Royal Hotel. My name is James; what's yours and what does such a beautiful girl like you, do out here in the sticks?'

'Thank you, I also live here, and my name is Sarah,' she replied, her smooth voice brimming with amusement.

Goodness, I thought, what a lovely voice; I bet she could also sing well, maybe to me one day. Plucking up all the courage I could summon, I asked if I could see her after I finished work at 1 pm; this being a Saturday, we only worked half a day.

Sarah answered, 'I would like to, but may I phone you later to confirm if it's possible?'

A brush-off, I thought, to be expected from such a beautiful girl.

Never mind, I was proud that at least I tried. Nevertheless, each time the phone rang that morning, my heart missed another beat, thinking *just maybe.*

Work that day was the last thing in my thoughts and suffered greatly. All I could think of was Sarah. What a lovely name she had, I thought. James and Sarah, they do go together well. Dream on, I thought, prepare yourself for another rejection.

At around 11 am, the phone rang again, and I somehow knew it was her. I simply melted into nothing hearing her voice as I nervously listened to her, expecting the worst. Contrary to my fears, she suggested that we meet at 2 pm at Father Eric's place. He was the local Catholic priest living in the rectory.

Clive, while waiting to start his training at the monastery, also had a room there and I always found it amusing how he would go from behind the hotel bar straight to the rectory.

The day dragged on and each minute ticked by slowly until closing time. At 1 pm, with my work half-finished, I grabbed my belongings and set off to the hotel. I had lunch and changed into something more casual, ready to meet Sarah.

In my haste, I nearly knocked myself out colliding with the front door of the hotel. I tried to act normal as I crossed the veranda and walked past the public bar, knowing that all eyes would be on me, I felt foolish, I bet they were all wondering where I was off to on foot.

I must have done the short walk to the rectory in Olympic time, even allowing the concerted effort put into trying to look normal. To my surprise Sarah was already there when I arrived, sitting on a bench in the rectory's shaded garden. My heart pounded. Was she as keen as me, or was that merely wishful thinking?

I eagerly joined her but taken in by her beauty; I didn't know what to say until she broke the ice, saying, 'Do you like living here? Judging by appearance, you don't seem like the outdoor farming type to me. I would have thought you are more an academic person, suited for city life. I do prefer a more refined type of man.'

Eager to please, I replied, 'You are right, although I like fishing and scuba diving. I probably would not make a great outdoor huntsman or farmer. Brought up in the city, and because I am single, they posted me here. Life here has been incredibly boring until this meeting with you. But what brings a beautiful girl like you to this village in the outback?'

Sarah's face turned serious and, twitching her nose a little. She replied, 'I live with my parents, who run a trading store not far out of town. For most of my life,

I have been attending boarding school in Maseru and only came home during school holidays. Now I am trying to decide what to do with my future, which does not include living here forever. In the meantime, I am helping my father, who also does the books for our local wholesaler.'

We carried on chatting in general about everything but honestly nothing at all. What I did learn was that Sarah's father was her adopted father. Sadly, before we could make any development in our friendship, the sound of a car horn broke the spell and Sarah had to leave.

'Can I see you again?' I got in quickly before she stood up to go.

Again, looking notably pensive, she twirled the ends of her hair. 'Monday at 5 pm, if that suits you. My father works a couple of hours' overtime every day, and I could get a lift with him. Please don't tell anyone about our meeting as I don't want my mom to find out from someone else. I am supposed to be practising the piano here at the rectory. I will tell her as soon as I know where our friendship is going.'

Delighted with her response, I must have grinned from ear to ear. 'I will be thrilled to see you on Monday. Please tell your mom soon; I want to tell the whole world how lucky I am meeting you.'

With that, she ran to her father's car. I tried to see what her father looked like, but it was difficult to tell from a distance. The car, however, was a recent model white Opel Record, but dusty. It didn't mean anything as most of the vehicles in town were dusty due to the dirt roads.

I floated back to the hotel with my head in the clouds, and chatted to Clive in the bar, dying to question him about Sarah since he lived in the rectory. I had to restrain myself not to mention a word of my good fortune in meeting her, frightened that this amazing bubble would burst and that this relationship would end before it had even started.

The most important topic of conversation in the bar was about the four German divers and their search for the *Grosvenor* treasure. There was in-depth speculation about how much treasure there was and if it was still possible to find it after all these years. Some proclaimed that it had shifted with the movement of the sand and now in a completely different place.

CHAPTER FIVE

Sunday must have been the longest day I had experienced in my life. I could not focus on anything and found myself bored with everything I attempted to do. Too scared to meet up with my friends as the only thing on my mind was Sarah. I did not want to discuss her with anyone as I promised not to talk about our friendship until she had told her parents.

Even the Germans had gone away for the weekend, and Clive was tending the bar. I consoled myself drinking beer and smoking one cigarette after the other, wondering if I should drive out to the trading store and ask to see Sarah. I dismissed this out of fear of upsetting her.

It seemed it took ages for Monday to arrive and work that day was dreadfully dull. I could not wait for 5 pm; then I could rush to the rectory for our meeting.

The rectory was a white single-story house with five bedrooms and a veranda along the front and the side of the house. A red corrugated iron roof protected it from the elements. The garden on the veranda side of the house had a lovely shaded area provided by two jacaranda trees.

The jacaranda tree is found throughout South Africa and is indeed magnificent. It has large compound leaves and adorned with purple blooms with a hint of fragrance in the spring and early summer. These blooms are shed in the autumn, creating a purple blanket on the ground. People believed that these trees bring good luck, especially when one of the flowers falls on your head.

A bougainvillaea hedge protected the garden from the street. It enhanced the tranquillity of the garden and created a peaceful secluded space. Two benches were positioned under the jacaranda trees to take advantage of the shade, and that is where we met.

When I arrived at the rectory after work, she was again waiting on a bench. As I approached her, I thought she was the most beautiful girl I had ever seen in my life.

Sarah greeted me with a warm smile. 'Hi, James, how are you?'

'I'm fine. Thank you. I hope you have not been waiting long. You look beautiful in that outfit.'

Sarah was wearing a long flared skirt with a white blouse and unobtrusive gold earrings. Her hair was woven into a plait and fastened with a tortoiseshell clasp.

'I missed you Sunday. Today took forever to pass, and work was boring.'

Sarah, twitching her nose, replied, 'I missed you too.'

I looked at Sarah and met her eyes, which were full of laughter and happiness. It was the type of look that would have awoken interest in me if I'd spotted it among others.

It encouraged me to take her hand in mine, sending electric shocks throughout my body. I could tell from the look in her eyes that it had the same effect on her. We sat quietly holding hands, each thrilling with the contact.

Her father's arrival, signalled by the sound of his car horn, ended an intensely intimate moment. To me, the feel of her hand was like an electric current that I thought would stay with me forever.

I was over the moon and could not believe my luck that such a beautiful girl could be interested in me.

There had to be a catch somewhere. Why would such a beautiful girl be interested in me, I am no mister universe or even wealthy, but an ordinary young man working as a clerk in the Post Office. Maybe the jacaranda trees were working their magic.

It was painful to wait until the next afternoon to see her again. I could not erase from my mind her lovely face with its slightly upturned nose and welcoming smile.

We continued seeing each other every afternoon, and our relationship soon progressed to kissing and cuddling. Our first kiss was intense and wanting. Soon it became gentler and loving. For me, kissing Sarah was pure heaven. Her lips were soft; it felt like they were melting on mine, and her body felt full of desire. It was a strain to pull away from her; I knew then that she was indeed the girl for me. Our friendship was becoming intense, and we both could feel the warmth of our desire for each other.

I could feel that Sarah was still holding back a bit and could not understand why.

It was about a week after this that Father Eric called us into the rectory for a chat.

'Sarah asked me to help her in explaining a few things, but I couldn't help noticing that the two of you were kissing and cuddling. Please don't think that I disapprove, for how could I when two people are infatuated with each other. Sarah is especially dear to me, and therefore I must explain that what you are doing is against the law and someone else will notice and report you. Then all of us will be in big trouble.'

Dropping this bombshell caught me entirely by surprise. I did not know to what Father Eric was referring. 'We were not doing anything wrong,' I spluttered, guiltily wondering if he noticed me fondling her breast, but without a doubt, that was not illegal?

'No, not in the eyes of our Lord, but the law of the land does not allow relationships across the colour bar,' he responded.

Still confused, I stammered, 'But we are both white.'

All this time, Sarah sat quietly, not saying a word as her eyes filled with tears.

She started explaining hesitantly, 'I wanted to tell you, but could not gather the courage. My mother is coloured, and my natural father was a white man from Switzerland. I love my mother, and it is not her fault, but because of this, the government has classified us all as non-white. That's why I didn't want you to tell anyone about our friendship.'

Sahra continued. 'Classified as a non-white person has been confusing to me since childhood. I spent my days playing with the black kids in front of the trading store. They were kind to me but would never treat me as their equal or take me into their confidence. I think being white made them feel that they should treat me with some superiority. When going to town, I was not allowed near the white kids who pulled faces and sneered at me as if I was some kind of trash.'

My heart cried out for Sarah as coloureds, described as racial misfits, once dismissed by the wife of the president, as 'non-persons...the leftovers.'

The skin tone of people of colour ranged from very pale to the darkest brown; many coloureds were (and still are) indistinguishable from their white or black compatriots. Some crossed the racial divide and became assimilated into white communities. But, after a ban on interracial sex in 1950, this became much more difficult. Borderline cases became subject to an infamous test. The curliness of someone's hair, a supposed indicator of blackness, was judged by inserting a pencil. If it slid out, the person in question was declared white.

The Group Areas Act barred non-white people from many urban and municipal areas. If the police saw you in the wrong part of a segregated park or beach, you would be questioned and given a warning.

I tried to stop Sarah from continuing to torture herself; she was now somewhat upset trying to account for herself, but she continued:

'I lived with my parents and half-brother Michael at the Qaukeni trading store near the village. The property was a smallholding of about twenty-five acres of woodland, with our house located behind the store.

From an early age, I spent hours exploring, climbing trees and riding her favourite horse, Prince. The family's two spaniel dogs always accompanied us. Michael, my brother, was a bit younger and learned all his woodland skills from me. He followed me around like a puppy dog when he was a toddler, and a close bond existed between the two of us.

My mother tried to no avail to mould me into a lady and was pleased when it was time for me to enrol at boarding school, hoping that my time as a tomboy was over. The boarding school was a private Catholic girl's school in Maseru, Lesotho.

At first, even the Catholic nuns seemed not to influence me. Immediately on my arrival home for holidays, I would be off to the woods with my horse and the two dogs. My favourite place was the little stream that meandered through the forest on our smallholding. I was particularly fond of visiting the creek at sunrise to watch the monkeys turning over rocks, looking for crabs and insects.

I could spend hours merely watching small animals and birds. I found that if one sat dead, still they would come real close to you. A duiker, a small, skittish antelope, came within touching distance once.

My obsession with animals and the forest was due to not being entirely accepted by other children. In appearance, I was white, the consequence of a prohibited relationship between my coloured mother and a white Swiss national. The black children found me to be white, and the white children's parents would not allow them to mix with me, classified as non-white.

This isolated lifestyle was not uncommon amongst the coloured community. Being rejected by both whites and blacks, definitely being born as the result of a crime, it did not offer many options.

It all changed after some time at the boarding school in Maseru, Lesotho. I began to love my time there; everyone treated as equal, and there were only kids, no matter if they were black or white. No one admitted or seemed to be of mixed colour, and we all played together in perfect harmony.

But sadly, this also changed as we got older. Even though there were no racial laws, the white kids would group, and the black kids would also have their group. We coloured kids were not accepted by either, and although we did mix, you knew that you were not part of either group.

I tried to mix with the white kids due to my pale complexion, but I felt not wanted by the tell-tale signs of conversations ending or changing the minute I joined their company. Although I missed my mother a lot, I dreaded going home during school holidays, having to face the reality of home life in South Africa as a coloured.'

Lesotho offered much freedom; it is a pity that there was no work as the country depended on foreign aid. Except for the people wanted by the police in South Africa for not adhering to the apartheid laws, or being members of the banned ANC, most worked in South Africa.

Sarah continued, 'As it was an all-girls school, experiences with the opposite sex were exceedingly rare and only in my mid-teens was I introduced to boys when we went to watch and support our local football team. After the match, a group of us got together, where I met Raymond. He was a white farmer's son from a village in South Africa, near the border of Lesotho and attended a boys' school in Maseru.

We met after that a few times, always at football matches as he was an exceptionally keen sportsman. Although we were friends, we differed a lot. I was more musical and loved to play the piano and he, well, he lived for his football. I also knew that although it was completely legal in Lesotho, he would probably not want to continue our friendship if he found out that I was coloured.

The apartheid laws were extremely efficient; they even influenced one's mindset in Lesotho, and soon I was branded as chasing white boys. Boys and sex were leading topics of conversation amongst us girls in the student house, but I had no such feelings towards Raymond.

I finished my education and had to leave the relative safety of my boarding school to return to South Africa and the reality that I was a second-class citizen.

My mental seclusion became more serious, and I wondered if I would ever make friends or even have a love affair. Being white made me feel more empathy towards whites, and I felt dejected when white people would not accept me because of my mixed heritage.

These feelings slowly built up to a passionate dislike of the government and the people of the country. My mother tried to calm my fears by assuring me that they were putting money aside every month to help me to leave the country. I started to dislike even the trading store, finding it dirty and noisy.

Life seemed to drag on at a slow pace with nothing exciting happening to me until I met you in front of the post office. From the first encounter, I felt warmth towards you and tried to work on an excuse to meet you again.

I was aware that you did not realise that I am coloured. It was not my intention to deceive you, but I was scared to tell you and end this nice feeling I got inside me every time we met. I did not think that the danger of illegal love influenced this feeling I had for you as it was the furthest thing from my mind.

The truth of the matter was that it was easier to ignore the consequences and hope for the best.'

Seeing the painful expression on Sarah's face, I took her in my arms and tried to soothe her, reassuring her of my love and that together we would face whatever turmoil may be ahead. Easier said than done; I was no hero and would typically run a mile, but the thought of losing Sarah, gave me courage.

I did not know whether to laugh or cry. It was a real mess, and although I did not want to break the law, I was quite sure that I was deeply in love with Sarah. The circumstances might also explain why such a beautiful girl was keen to see me. Hopefully, I was not regarded by Sarah as her ticket out of here.

Interrupting my thoughts, Father Eric explained, 'Racial segregation is implemented and enforced by a large number of acts and other laws. This legislation institutionalises racial discrimination and assures dominance by white people over people of different races.

It also legalised the racial segregation of public premises, vehicles and services. In practice, the best facilities were reserved for whites, while those for other races were inferior.'

'What if we were to get married, that is, if Sarah agrees?' I requested feebly.

Father Eric interrupted, 'No, you can't. I can see you both love each other, and I am not going to stand in your way. However, if you are going to continue with this relationship, I suggest you take great care to avoid public places. In future, meet inside the rectory instead. Sarah can always make the excuse that she is practising on the piano, which is not a lie as she should exercise her musical talents more.

James, you will have to create your deception and reasons for coming here. Maybe Clive could help. But please take great care or else we will all be in trouble. Also, if possible, refrain from having sex as there are even more significant penalties enforcing this law; punishable as an act of immorality by the government.'

'We can't get married, or seen together, and we can't have sex. What happens if caught?' I enquired pathetically.

Father Eric explained, 'The Immorality Act that prohibited sex between white people and any non-white person is subject to a penalty of up to five years in prison for the man and four years for the woman. It also prohibited to allow premises to be used for interracial sex knowingly; this offence carries a penalty of up to five years imprisonment.'

He continued, 'The truly frightening thing about these laws is knowing you are friendly with the magistrate and all the police here in town, I am sure that they will not pursue you. It is the ordinary people in the town of whom you must take care. If one person complains or reports you, the police have to act as it is their duty and it is straightforward for them to prosecute you. The mere fact that the two of you are alone in the same room is enough evidence to convict you.'

With that, he left us alone to contemplate the frightful situation we were in, naturally, wanting to be a hero, I immediately expressed my feelings by telling Sarah that I did not want to lose her and would like to continue meeting. I was sure that a solution to this, which was only a minor problem compared to the love I felt for her, would be found soon.

Secretly, I was petrified of the whole situation and could not think how to resolve the predicament we found ourselves. All I knew was that I loved Sarah dearly and could not simply walk away.

It was insane, I thought. It was not my intention to become a criminal. Unquestionably falling in love was second only to breathing, and if that is a crime, what are we to do?

CHAPTER SIX

If you are conversant with the apartheid laws of South Africa, you may want to skip this chapter and move on straight to chapter seven. Otherwise, it will benefit you better to understand the coloured population's position in South Africa.

You have to investigate back into the centuries, to understand the current law as enacted by the white minority government.

Discrimination against non-white people dates back before South Africa even became a republic. As far back as 1797, when it was still only a settlement, pass laws existed to control the movement of non-whites. The British colonial government affirmed this. To move to a different area, the coloured resident would have to get a pass from their master or a local official. They only issued passes for seeking work.

The relations between races were regulated, and legislation used to limit the freedom of non-whites. It happened throughout the nineteenth century in all the colonies of South Africa. It became known as the Pass System, limiting them to fixed areas.

With the creation of the Union of South Africa in 1910, this programme of racial regulation continued. The white race gained complete political control over all other racial groups, and they abolished the rights of non-whites to sit in parliament.

Over time, even more, bills were passed, which included residential segregation. Non-whites moved into locations on the edge of town, providing cheap labour for an industry owned by white people and prevented black workers from practising skilled trades.

Continuing with this trend, the British Crown, instead of the paramount chiefs, became the head of all African affairs. These bills were accepted by the majority of white South Africa even though it was clear that the opportunities and rights for whites and non-whites were not equal.

There was no planning for the accommodation of a large number of black workers needed in the industrial cities to replace the wartime shortage of white labour. It led to a housing shortage, and overcrowding resulted in an increased crime rate. In turn, this caused disillusionment. Many urban blacks now supported movements that advocated the principle of self-determination and freedom, as stated in the Atlantic Charter.

These changes, as well as the superior power and prosperity of the English, did not go down well with most Afrikaners. The National Party, although only a small minority party, offered the voters a new policy to ensure white supremacy. They proposed to make the relations, rights and privileges of the races into law.

Segregation, only enforced by local society such as separate schools, instead of being imposed as a law. They now proposed to include all these bills under a new law named apartheid. Although it meant 'separate development', it was an unfortunate choice of name for this policy, as in English it is pronounced as 'apart- hate'.

The National Party won the 1948 election with a commanding majority and implemented the apartheid policy, thus silencing the liberal opposition. The government now passed laws to establish grand apartheid. It centred on the large-scale separation of the races. People, compelled to live in separate places as defined by their race created Black-only townships.

Racial classification was the first grand apartheid law. This required identity cards for all persons over the age of eighteen that specified their racial groups. The population was classified into four groups: black, white, Asian, and coloured. The Coloured group included people regarded as being of mixed descent, including those brought to South Africa from other parts of the world. Boards would decide on the classification of those people whose race was unclear, creating difficulties for people of colour, with some families forced to separate due to being allocated to different races.

Then they introduced the Group Areas Act. Until then, most settlements had people of different races living side by side. This Act put an end to it. Each ethnic group received its area which, in later years, was used as a basis for forced removal.

The government introduced new laws known as 'petty apartheid'. These laws include the ban of marriages between persons of different races. Sexual relations with a person of another race became a criminal offence.

Municipal grounds reserved for a particular race under the Reservation of Separate Amenities Act. They were creating separate beaches, buses, hospitals, schools, and universities. Signboards such as 'whites-only' were applied to public areas and even included park benches. Blacks and people of mixed race received services inferior to those of whites.

Public beaches also separated by race, the beach facilities for non-whites were few and far between. Segregation applied to swimming pools, graveyards, parks, and public toilets, as well as some pedestrian bridges and drive-in cinemas too. In most of these cases, there were hardly any facilities for non-whites.

Laws introduced aimed at suppressing resistance, especially armed resistance, to apartheid were passed. Communism and parties supporting it were banned. Communism, defined in general terms that anyone who opposed government policy risked labelled a communist. Communism used to gag the opposition to apartheid. Disorderly gatherings were banned, including organisations considered to be threatening to the government.

Education, divided into separate systems. School for blacks designed to prepare them for lives as a labouring class.

Before the introduction of the apartheid government's Bantu Education Act, 90% of black South African schools were state-aided mission schools. The Act demanded that all such schools register with the state and removed control of African education from the churches and provincial authorities. This control was centralised in the Bantu Education Department, a body dedicated to keeping it separate and inferior. Almost all the mission schools closed down. The Roman Catholic Church was mostly alone in its attempt to keep its schools going without state aid. The Act also separated the financing of education for Africans from general state spending. It linked it to direct tax paid by Africans themselves, with the result that they spent far less on black children than on white children.

Expenditure on Bantu Education increased from the late 1960s, once the apartheid Nationalist government saw the need for a trained African labour force. Through this, more African children attended school than under the old missionary system of education, albeit grossly deprived of facilities in comparison with the teaching of other races, especially whites.

Nationally, pupil: teacher ratios went up from 46:1 in 1955 to 58:1 in 1967. Overcrowded classrooms got used on a rota basis. There was also a lack of teachers, and many of those who did teach were underqualified. In 1961, only 10 per cent of black teachers held a matriculation certificate [last year of high school]. Black education was essentially retrogressing, with teachers being less qualified than their students.

The Coloured Person's Education Act of 1963 put control of 'coloured' education under the Department of Coloured Affairs. 'Coloured' schools also had to be registered with the government. 'Coloured' education was made compulsory but was now effectively separated from white schooling.

The government created separate structures for blacks and whites. It was the first piece of legislation supporting the government's plan of independent development in the Bantu homelands, which would have devolved administrative powers.

The government planned to grant independence to these homelands in later years. These plans, justified on the basis that the government's policy was not discrimination on the grounds of race or colour, but a system based on the grounds of different nations. Each nation was to be granted self-determination within the borders of their homelands, hence the policy of separate development. Under the homelands system, blacks would no longer be citizens of South Africa, but citizens of their independent territories. They then worked in South Africa as foreign migrant labourers on temporary work permits. The Transkei was one of these homelands.

Non-whites could not run businesses or professional practices in areas nominated as white South Africa unless they had a permit. They were required to move to areas allocated to them or the black homelands, setting up businesses and practices there.

The government separated white and non-white transport and public facilities. Buses for non-whites stopped at non-white bus stops and buses for whites at white ones. The same applied to trains, hospitals and ambulances.

Non-whites, excluded from living or working in white areas unless they had a pass, issued only to a non-white with approved work.

Non-whites could not apply for work in white areas unless they had a pass. It created a continuous loop of illegality. Many white homeowners got punished for employing non-white servants and giving them living quarters in their back garden, thus breaking the pass law.

Spouses and children left behind in their designated areas or black homelands. A pass to non-whites for work was issued for one town, confining the holder to that area only. Being without a valid pass made a person subject to arrest and prosecuted for breaking the pass laws.

People of colour who used to live in white areas had to move to mixed-race zones, which were usually in locations on the edge of white towns. Mixed-race people could not settle in the black homelands.

White towns surrounded all the black territories, as they represented massive trading opportunities. Lusikisiki was no different. A small white village with several farms, it was surrounded by a sizeable Bantu homeland and part of the Transkei. There was no location for people of colour due to their limited numbers. They lived in inferior houses on the edge of town.

Apartheid law grew to become part of the culture and established itself in most of the mainstream media.

Cinemas and theatres in white areas were not allowed to admit non-whites. There were hardly any cinemas in non-white neighbourhoods. Non-whites were not allowed in most restaurants or hotels, except as staff.

Voting rights denied to coloureds in the same way as denied to blacks.

Non-whites could never buy land in white areas. In the black homelands, the land belonged to the tribe. Permission about the use of the property rested in the control of the local chieftain. As a result of this, the whites owned almost all the industrial and agricultural land. They also claimed most of the prized residential areas.

Being brought up under the influence of these discriminating laws, Sarah, classified as a non-white, found it difficult to meet friends, making her into a bit of a recluse. However, she found some consolation in singing in the church choir and playing the piano. Non-white people were also excluded from white churches by law, but the local Catholic churches ignored these rules.

At first, Sarah found it difficult to understand that her father and her brother Michael had a dark skin and her mother was sort of in-between. Sarah herself was completely white. As Sarah grew older, her mother explained to her that her biological father was a white man from Switzerland. He was no longer in contact with them, and she had no idea where he was.

Mr Meth, who adopted her as his own, was her stepfather and the biological father of Michael, her brother. Making it more complicated for Sarah to comprehend: even though her skin is white, she is still classified as coloured. The irony is that if classified as white, she would not be able to live with her family.

The apartheid bureaucracy devised intricate criteria at the time of the Population Registration Act implementation to determine who was coloured. Minor officials would administer tests to determine if someone should be categorised either coloured or black, or if another person should be categorised either coloured or white. Different members of the same family could find themselves in different race groups.

One of these tests was the famous pencil test. A pencil was inserted into your hair if it fell out you were white, if not you were non-white.

The sad thing was that every person of colour was the result of a crime, as sexual relations between black and white was against the law. Therefore, the mother and the father of the coloured child would have to live separate lives.

Discriminated against by apartheid, coloureds were, as a matter of state policy, forced to live in separate townships, in some cases leaving homes their families had occupied for generations, and received an inferior education, though better than that provided to blacks. They played an essential role in the anti-apartheid movement: for example, the

African People's Organization (APO) established in 1902 had an exclusively coloured membership.

Investigations found that the board created no benefit at all for students who were coloured. The APO lobbied the board and thus established the first school for coloured children. Trafalgar High School, created as a direct result of damning criticism of the Cape School Board in the APO newspaper in August 1911.

The APO represented South African coloured protest politics until its demise in 1923 while also publishing a significant newspaper called *the APO*.

CHAPTER SEVEN

We agreed to continue with our friendship allowing the relationship to blossom and grow, even if this led to making love. Father Eric should not have mentioned the word 'sex' as it now stuck in my mind, and all my thoughts revolved around it. I could not help imagining her beautiful naked body in my arms.

Lusikisiki was a small town full of busybodies interfering in everyone's private affairs. Boredom and the fact that all the residents were living in each other's pockets was the driving force. Conducting an illicit affair under these circumstances was incredibly tricky, very scary and bordered on the impossible.

I do not know, from where my courage came. I can only assume that my love for Sarah drove it. We continued seeing each other daily at the rectory. I achieved this by me sneaking out the back of the hotel. My room was at the end of a long passage, and opposite was the back door leading to a vegetable garden. Crossing this you came to a field that joined the rear of the rectory garden. I followed this route every afternoon.

On each of these trips, my stomach felt all tied up in knots. I had the feeling that the whole world was watching, knowing exactly where I was going—with a rigid gait, looking all around, especially behind me. I made my way to the rectory, hoping that I am unobserved, it was difficult, especially since the parsonage was a public place and all sorts of people came to see Father Eric for all kinds of different reasons.

On one such occasion, the police arrived. I dived out the window while Sarah innocently continued playing the piano. Fortunately, they only wanted Father Eric's help in locating a person.

On another occasion, the magistrate was visiting Father Eric, and I had to make the excuse that I was looking for Clive while knowing full well that Clive was working in the hotel at that time.

On each of these occasions, I ended up shaking uncontrollably, my nerves shattered. As I said, I was no hero, my infatuation for Sarah driving me.

All this cloak and dagger stuff fuelled our relationship to become an intense courtship. The illegality of our meetings made everything scary but more exciting, and our embraces became more passionate as if there was no tomorrow.

Our courtship built up to such a fervour that making love was almost impossible to avoid. We both decided that this is what we wanted and started making plans to go someplace where it would be safe without being observed.

The rectory was not the place for privacy as both Father Eric and Clive were continuously interrupting us; this was done on purpose to prevent something like that happening. I could not sneak her into my hotel room; this would be enormously risky and probably impossible to achieve.

During my visits to the rectory, Sarah regularly played the piano, especially when Father Eric or Clive were present. I could only watch her at the piano in the semi-darkness of the room, admiring her gentle profile. Her face gained colour from her pleasure in the music, and sometimes she would also sing while playing. The first time I heard her sing, it was one of my favourites, 'You've got a friend' by Carole King. As she finished her song, Sarah's voice died away into the silence of the house, and she dropped her fingers from the keys and sat there motionless.

'That was simply beautiful,' I marvelled.

She turned to me, her eyes shining in the dim light. 'You genuinely thought that it was nice?'

Clive interrupted, 'Your voice is like an angel singing from above. I can now see why you two are taking these tremendous risks, continuing this relationship.'

I desperately wanted to tell Sarah that her voice was beautiful and that I loved her incredibly much but was frustrated that there was always company to interrupt these special moments. I could only agree and added that the unique, soft quality of her voice was magical, and she should develop it even further as she was fit to perform on stage.

Her talents as a singer remain wasted, while regarded as a non-person in this country. The ladder of success for a talented young person of mixed race was stunted in this country by the white government cutting up the rungs. Even then, in my mind, I thought that England could be the solution to all our problems as I had a British passport.

A month passed before I hatched a plan for us to get away. On Sunday, Sarah would slip away on the pretext that she was going to church, and I would then drive her to Mboyti, where Clive's parents had a beach cottage they allowed me to use.

Sunday morning, I collected the food hamper, that I asked the hotel kitchen to prepare for my lunch and set off to pick up Sarah from the church, where her stepfather had dropped her.

The road to Mboyti was not indeed a road, but instead two poorly maintained tracks with no bridges but drifts to cross the numerous rivers. My car was of no use in these conditions; I had to borrow a pickup truck from Clive. He gladly agreed but added this comment, 'Please don't let Sarah sit in the front with you, especially near town. Somebody is bound to notice; they all know my pickup and are stupid enough to assume it was me driving. Being involved with the Catholic Church, the general public label me as being in sympathy with the blacks. The residents of our town, however friendly they seem, will not hesitate to report it to the police, who in turn will get overenthusiastic and arrest me on the spot.'

The Catholic Church condemned apartheid, proclaiming that no system of separate development will ever be acceptable as a model for the relations between peoples or races.

'Clive, one can't expect a lovely girl like Sarah to ride in the back of the pickup with all the black kids?' I questioned.

'Welcome to our world of state security. You have crossed the line by befriending Sarah, and the authorities will construe anything you do now as an act against the state. Lesson number one, don't trust anyone.'

His pickup was a used Datsun 520 without four-wheel drive. I collected Sarah from the trading store, and ashamedly I explained to her what Clive had warned and tried to make her as comfortable as possible in the back of the pickup. On the way, I also picked up as many Pondo kids as possible to take them with us for the drive. They loved it and were always eagerly waiting by the side of the road.

Looking at the bright, smiling faces of these black kids, they were friendly and unassuming it made me wonder if they were aware of the fact that they were slaves of the whites and had no opportunity to improve their status. The only choice open was to stay in the homelands in poverty or go to the cities as labourers.

After travelling some distance from town, Sarah joined me in the cab. She was impressed with my kindness for giving the black kids a day out. I explained to her that I thought they were fun to have around and, besides, loading them on the back gave the pickup truck more traction. If we got stuck, there were always plenty of helping hands to push.

The road was a poorly maintained single-lane gravel path not suitable for cars or two-wheel drive vehicles. In places, the grass was growing in the middle of the way with two tracks for the pickup's wheels.

The trip down was picturesque with rolling grassy hills but was slow and a bit hazardous in places with livestock—Nguni cattle herds and goats—grazing nose to tail. The local natives did not invest in fencing, and their cattle wandered all over the place. The road seemed to be their favourite place.

Nguni cattle are known for their fertility and resistance to diseases, being the favourite breed amongst the local Bantu-speaking people of South Africa. Characterised by their multicoloured skin, which can have many different patterns, but their noses are always black-tipped. These animals have a variety of horn shapes and are medium-sized, with bulls weighing between 500 kg and 600 kg, while cows weigh between 300 kg and 400 kg. The little pickup truck was no match for these cattle, and I had to drive with the utmost care, leaving the road in several places to avoid them.

While trying to light a cigarette for me, Sarah remarked, 'The countryside is lovely; it's a pity one can't enjoy the trip for this bumpy road.'

'Yes,' I responded, taking the cigarette from Sarah. 'The road is not going to attract tourists to such a lovely area. I suppose we should be grateful that today we are all by ourselves and do not to have to worry about who is looking.'

With that, Sarah's hand dropped to my leg, giving me a light squeeze. 'Yes, isn't it wonderful, the two of us going to the seaside like ordinary people. But seriously, what are we going to do? I do treasure every moment that we spend together, but I want more. I want to be with you whenever we choose, not this sneaking around to see each other.'

I replied, 'Make no mistake I have been giving this a lot of thought. It seems that we have only two choices. We can try to get you reclassified as white, but that is problematic. There is no guarantee that this would succeed, and if it does, your mother and your brother will have to live separate from you and, even then, will all these fascist-white people accept you? If it does not work, you will be a marked person, and our relationship will be even more precarious.

In my mind, the only real solution is for us to move to the United Kingdom. I have a British passport, and it will not be difficult for us to settle there as ordinary people. The only thing we need is money, which we don't have at the moment. Perhaps I should ask my parents for a loan. It may be a solution, although I was hoping for us to do something like this with their blessings but our own money. Anyway, let's not worry too much about that today; it is our first day out together without an escort.'

Sarah grinned at me. 'Okay, not another word, it is only that we never seem to get the opportunity to have a serious conversation.'

'Or a serious cuddle,' I replied, grinning from ear to ear.

Sarah moved closer to me and rested her head on my shoulder. 'I do love you incredibly much and pray every night that everything will turn out roses for us.'

'I love you too, and I am positive we will succeed. I simply don't know how at this moment. Look! I saw the sea,' I beamed, pointing.

The rolling grassy hills were now replaced with shrubs and woodland as we approached the coastline; soon we reached the Mboyti river mouth, near where the beach cottage was situated. Mboyti was dreadfully isolated but astonishingly beautiful, with a lovely sandy beach. I was quite sure nobody would disturb us here.

The cottage was a log cabin consisting of a bedroom, a lounge with a kitchen area, and a bathroom. A small Honda petrol generator supplied the electricity. You had to fetch water in buckets from the Mboyti River; knowing this, I had brought a container of water from the hotel.

The front of the cabin featured a raised platform that sat above the dense scrubs, planted to protect the cabin from the encroaching sand. It looked out to the sea and the gentle waves that rolled on to the unspoiled sandy beach.

On arrival, I showed Sarah the cottage, told the kids to unload all the gear and then to scatter, but to return for lunch at about two o'clock. How they managed to ascertain the time was a mystery as there was not a single watch amongst them.

Sarah and I walked to the small bay with its sandy beach near the cabin, surrounded by a coastline of green grassy cliffs. The sheer drama of the surroundings was both pleasant and wild and reminded me of pictures I had seen of Ireland, with the landscape, green and the sea, blue. In some areas, the grassy fields reached right to the edge of the sea, populated by comical goats, cows and even donkeys.

Sitting on some driftwood logs, we contemplated life while our feet paddled in the sea's warm water. 'I could stay here forever with you by my side. Don't you think it's beautiful?' I commented.

'Yes, it's lovely. Look at the lovely lagoon!' Sarah exclaimed, pointing to the right at the broad estuary of the Mboyti River. It sparkled turquoise in the sunlight and was teeming with life; she dragged me excitedly towards it to better view the large variety of birds and butterflies. Sarah spotted some white pelicans nesting on the lagoon, sharing the water with mallard ducks, geese, many kinds of kingfishers, and fish eagles busy fishing.

'Isn't it simply lovely here? Should we go for a swim before lunch? The water looks inviting,' I asked.

'Yes, let's do,' Sarah responded.

We ran back to the cottage to change into our swimming gear and found that the owners of the cabin conveniently left several pairs of fins, goggles and snorkels. 'What a lovely surprise!' Sarah exclaimed delightfully.

We both liked diving, and keenly wanted to explore the ocean as well as the lagoon. Diving in the Wild Coast is an experience to savour. The edge of the continental shelf lies closer to the Wild Coast than anywhere else in South Africa. The region is therefore affected by the Agulhas current, which brings warm, tropical water down the coast. At the same time, seasonal fluctuations cause a colder counter-current to move north, bringing temperate water species into the area.

Sarah, in her swimming costume, was a breath-taking sight. Her beautifully formed body with curves in the right places was another of nature's wonders. I found it difficult to avert my eyes from her body and tingled all over merely holding her hand. I had an overpowering feeling of wanting to take her in my arms to make love right there and then.

We made our way to the mouth of the estuary. The near side was smooth sand, but the opposite bank was extraordinarily rocky and looked like an exciting place to explore underwater. It was not very deep and ideal for snorkelling; as we entered the water, schools of young elf and grunter were all around us. We made our way to the rocks on the far bank which hosted barnacles, limpets, periwinkles and several species of algae.

It grew more abundant in animal and plant life the more down we went, with colourful sponges, green algae, coral-like seaweeds, and mussels dominating our view. Below the low-tide mark offered the most exceptional diversity, with animals such as red bait, anemones, sea urchins, starfish and fish such as blacktail, zebra and karanteen competing for our attention. There were also many plants, including colourful branched seaweeds and kelp, and an abundance of rock lobster living in the crevices and holes under the rocks.

After about an hour of exploring, we returned to the sandy side of the shore and lay their side by side, holding hands and taking in the sun. 'This is the most beautiful experience I had in my life, all the different fish and plants,' Sarah murmured lazily.

'For me too, also being with the most beautiful girl in the world,' I remarked, taking her into my arms.

For the first time in our relationship, I felt free from the fear of being observed and kissed her with all the passion I could gather. Sarah responded with equal pleasure, and soon I was embracing her naked body against mine and fondling her firm breasts. She guided me into her, willing me to thrust ever deeper until we both climaxed with pleasure more magnificent than I had ever imagined.

Afterwards, we lay spent in each other's arms, and I thought I could do this every day forever. I was lucky to have such a beautiful and loving girl.

We returned to the cabin and shared our barbeque lunch with the Pondo kids, tidied up the cabin, and too soon we were on our way back to town.

After that, every Sunday, we would be off to the cottage, both eagerly awaiting our lovemaking. After which we spent hours walking hand in hand exploring the beach, carefree in the thought that we were far from civilisation and nobody could spoil our love for each other. Life was one continuous ecstasy and I could not bear the daily separation between us, wanting to spend every minute with Sarah.

CHAPTER EIGHT

By this time, Sarah had told her parents about our relationship as she was fearful that they would find out from someone else. They were exceptionally friendly with Father Eric as they were also Catholic.

Apartheid had a significant impact on women of colour since they suffered both racial and gender discrimination. Jobs were often hard to find. Many coloured women worked as agricultural or domestic workers, but wages were meagre.

Children in non-white families tended to suffer from diseases caused by malnutrition and sanitation problems, and mortality rates were high. The controlled movement of black and coloured workers within the country and the pass laws separated family members from one another. Men usually worked in urban centres while women were forced to stay in the fringes of small rural towns, basically imprisoning them in the areas from where they originated.

This discrimination and poverty contributed to the motivation of women of colour to form relationships with white European men as to a means to escape this financial trap, especially amongst women of colour with lighter skin.

In an attempt to protect Sarah, they sent her to a Catholic boarding school in Maseru, Lesotho where there was no racial discrimination. She was one of the fortunate ones, whose parents could afford boarding school.

It was her first exposure to the real world after boarding school. Classified as a non-white with white skin in South Africa was a difficult situation because she didn't fit in on either side of the racial line. Indeed, her only solution would be to leave the country, but now there was me creating all sorts of problems.

Our situation did not endear me to her mother and stepfather. I met them for the first time at Sarah's insistence on a Sunday; sacrificing our day at Mboyti, I drove out to the trading store owned by her parents.

Sarah's mother also had a pale complexion, although nowhere near as white as Sarah's. Her younger brother, Michael, and Mr Meth, her adopted father, were much darker and definitely could not pass as white. He was a friendly man, and we hit it off from the start, speaking endlessly about bookkeeping as we shared this common interest.

Mrs Meth was a bit reserved, but I thought it was due to her fear that life was repeating itself, and Sarah would end up in the same position as her: having a child with a white man, who would then pack his bags and disappear.

The conversation led to discussing ancestors, and it came out that Sarah's mother was related to the survivors of the *Grosvenor* wreck. I told them about the four Germans living at the hotel who were trying to salvage the treasure, and Mr Meth laughed, saying that they would never find it as they were diving in the wrong place.

Alone in my room that evening, I enjoyed a double whisky and reflected on the events taking place in my life. I thought that if I had any sense, now would be an excellent time to make a run for it as I feared that trouble was around the corner and heading my way.

My typical instinct as I dislike confrontation of any sort would be to remove myself from the danger looming on the horizon. I have never been one for heroics and could not understand this force that was driving me forward to continue with this relationship. Surely it could not be lust. It had to be deeper than that.

The irony of the situation did not escape me. Here I was in love with this beautiful girl, who was probably whiter in colour than me, but who was not allowed to go to the same toilet or sit on the same park bench. Never mind having a sexual relationship with her. I felt as if being punished for Sarah having mixed blood.

Without commonly accepted rules about things like law or state, no complex human society can function. We can't play football unless everyone believes in the same made-up rules, and we can't enjoy the benefits of nationality and courts without similar made-up rules. But these rules are only tools. They shouldn't become our goals or our yardsticks, especially when a small minority of the population creates these rules as a means of protecting itself.

When we forget that these rules are mere fiction, we lose touch with reality—believing, for instance, that separating races on a large scale, by compelling people to live in separate places defined by race is right 'to protect the national interest'. Nations exist only in our imagination. We invented them to serve us; why then do we allow ourselves to become enslaved by them?

And this is the case in South Africa where the whole white nation has lost touch with reality. These apartheid laws were not adequately thought through and were incredibly cruel, especially to the coloured community.

I was going to have to do some careful planning if I wanted this relationship to continue to thrive without getting into serious trouble. Make no mistake; brought up with these laws and, to a certain extent, even in favour of separate development, being of the view that different races should be protected and allowed to retain their own cultures and values. They were trying to stop the toughest race exploiting the weakest.

The various tribes should be granted independence in their traditional homelands. It could not be applied to people of mixed race as they did not belong to any particular racial group and should merge into the rest of South Africa, where all of the people should be allowed to mix and have equal rights.

To punish and classify people for the deeds of their ancestors and not judge them by their character and conduct was not one of my views. I would be delighted to take Sarah to my parents' home and was sure my mother would love her for her enchanting character.

The apartheid laws were all good and well if you were white, but if not, they were unpleasant and cruel. We had a fascist society indeed, and I sometimes felt embarrassed to be part of it.

I started to notice that the regular crowd in the bar did not include me in darts or their conversation, except for the *Grosvenor*-seeking Germans. I also noticed that the usual noisy breakfast scenes had become a more low-spirited occasion when I was present.

Rumours were also spreading about the German divers, alleging that they were spies and signalling Russian fishing trawlers where to drop off terrorists and arms to aid the banned African National Congress, a political party in South Africa. The massacre of peaceful protestors and the subsequent banning of the ANC made it clear that peaceful protest alone would not force the regime to change.

The ANC went underground and continued to organise secretly. Umkhonto we Sizwe, Zulu for

'Spear of the Nation', co-founded by Nelson Mandela and abbreviated as MK, was formed to 'hit back by all means within our power in defence of our people, our future and our freedom.'

This underground organisation was no match for the government, which began to use even harsher methods of repression. The government introduced laws to make the death penalty the punishment for sabotage and to allow the police to detain people for 90 days without trial. In 1963, police raided the secret headquarters of MK, arresting their leaders.

After that, most of the ANC underground structures in the country was in ruin. The ANC question of how to bring trained soldiers and supplies back into the country to continue there struggle. However, South Africa now was surrounded by countries that were hostile to the ANC. It was clear that MK would have to find other ways to achieve their aims. It led to a campaign to promote international support and assistance, thus the allegations that the German divers were helping the ANC by being go-betweens with Russian fishing trawlers. In reality, anyone with overseas connections was a suspect.

I thought they seemed to be ordinary young guys, in search of adventure and trying to make money by looking for lost treasure. I was not sure if the locals thought that I was one of them, or perhaps something leaked out about Sarah and me, but I could sense that this was building up to something awful.

It all came to a head a few weeks later when security police or better known as BOSS, swarmed the hotel early one morning and arrested the four German divers. Where and why they went, nobody knew. The security police loaded them in their Land Rovers and sped away in a cloud of dust.

If someone suspected of involvement in terrorism, broadly defined as anything that might endanger the maintenance of law and order, the security police can detain him for a 90-day period, which they can renew without trial on the authority of a senior police officer. Since there was no requirement to release information about who they held, people detained tended to disappear. The law was utterly severe, giving the police draconian powers that they continuously misused against the black community.

Secretly I was relieved, as I feared that it could have been Sarah and me. It seemed that we were safe for the time being, and we could continue as usual.

I spent every waking moment thinking of a way that we could leave the country and escape the situation we found ourselves. But the big problem was always money. It was like a brick wall, obstructing our way forward.

CHAPTER NINE

After the arrest of the German divers, I thought back to the days when I used to dive for sinkers. Definitely diving for treasure must be similar. If I could only find some of it, all my problems would be solved. It must be worth a try, especially now that the Germans had left all their equipment behind. Besides, this could be an ideal opportunity and cover to spend more time with Sarah.

After serious consideration, I discussed this problem with Sarah's stepfather the next time I saw him. I suggested that the only future Sarah and I had as a couple would be to move to another country.

'To achieve this we would need money, more than what I was earning at present. If I could get permission to use the German divers' equipment, including their rubber dingy with an outboard motor, I could not see the harm in trying to find some of the lost treasure. We do, however, need your help in knowing exactly where to search as I recalled, you remark that the Germans were looking in the wrong place.'

'True,' he stated. 'I know an old man who knows the story well as it passed down through the generations. He states that he knows exactly where the *Grosvenor* wrecked itself against the rocks. Although this information is not common knowledge and the old man would not divulge this to anyone else, I am sure if I explained to him your situation, he would be willing to help. I mean since Sarah is descendant of the survivors, one could call it her inheritance.'

Mr Meth also told me that in 1880 Mr Turner tried to salvage the *Grosvenor* and found some treasure. He recovered some Indian coins and Venetian ducats as well as several cannons, two of them displayed at the local history museum in Durban. Then they also tried to build a harbour there, calling it *Port Grosvenor,* but by 1886 it had faded into obscurity.

We decided to meet the next Sunday with this old man who would take us to the exact place. The reason the local tribesmen had not tried searching for the wreck is that it is about 400m from the shore; they don't like swimming and were fearful of the strong currents. The rubber dingy was, therefore, a necessity.

I went to see the local magistrate to ask his opinion, and he stated that he could see no harm in trying, and suggested that I employed one of the local tribesmen to guard the equipment in case the Germans returned. If not, someone will steal all their gear. He also mentioned that if we found anything of historical value, it must be declared to him as we must process it as treasure trove.

That Sunday I set off in Clive's pickup, first collecting Sarah, her stepfather and brother Michael on the way to the Mkweni river mouth. The road was no better than the one to Mboyti, and again we picked up a load of black youths to take with us for the drive.

I thought that I must buy a pickup; my car was of no use out here on these tracks they called roads. Clive had agreed that I could buy his truck when he entered the monastery, but that was still months away. Maybe we could swap now? I wondered if they were allowed a car in the monastery.

To my dismay, Sarah and Michael had to sit in the back with the black children, while Mr Meth shared the cab with me. It always made me feel bad when Sarah had to sit in the rear; it was no place for such a lovely girl. Sarah, however, insisted that she was fine and did not mind the minor discomfort.

We could not truly converse during the trip as the road was extremely hazardous and full of wandering animals, which put Mr Meth on edge as he was a nervous passenger.

On arrival at the Mkweni river mouth, we immediately spotted the camp of the German divers. It was an especially pictures scene situated on the right bank of the river with the sea about fifty meters in front of us. The camp consisted of three tents, two small ones used for storing equipment, but in my eyes, suitable to use for sleeping and a large one used for storing provisions, equipment, and a table and chairs for meals.

Outside was a neatly organised barbeque built with bricks and a stockpile of charcoal covered by a tarp to keep it dry. On the river bank was the black rubber dingy and outboard motor, also covered with a canvas pegged into the ground.

Someone had thoroughly searched the camp. After inspection, we found that all seemed undamaged except that someone took all the provisions and beers.

It appeared that the intruders had a party, leaving food wrappers and beer bottles strewn all over the place.

Mr Meth left us to sort out the camp while he took the pickup to fetch his friend, the old man who knew the exact location of where we should search. He was also the head man in the area, and he could nominate a reliable person to watch over the camp.

Fortunately, I bought a can of fuel with as we soon discovered that there were no fuel or fuel cans to be found. Other than that, the rubber dingy seemed seaworthy and intact, starting the first time after I refuelled it.

We decided to give scuba diving a pass on this trip, which gave me time to first check over the oxygen tanks and equipment for safety. Mr Meth confirmed that he could have them filled and checked out at the wholesaler.

The term 'oxygen tank' is commonly used by non-divers; however, this is a misnomer since these cylinders typically contain (compressed atmospheric) breathing air, or an oxygen-enriched air mix. They rarely carry pure oxygen, except when used for rebreather diving, shallow decompression stops in technical diving or for in-water oxygen recompression therapy. Breathing pure oxygen at depths greater than 6 metres (20 ft) can result in oxygen toxicity.

Sarah's father arrived with his old friend, who must have been in his nineties. He had short, curly grey hair, and was thin and gaunt, with deep wrinkles on his face. He seemed shrivelled and bent, and the lines and scars on his hands showed decades of manual work. Everything about him was old: even his shirt had been patched many times and faded to many different shades by the sun. Yet his eyes were energetic, cheerful and undefeated. He gestured wildly that this was nowhere near the correct place; it was even on the wrong side of the river.

Without any further to do, he climbed into the dingy, demanding that we join him; we set off on the river and out to sea. He guided us to a spot about 500 meters north of the river and about 400 meters from the shore, indicating that this was the spot. I noticed we were on a rocky reef and that it was about knee-deep, but the current was powerful, making it challenging to keep the dingy steady.

I climbed over the side, keeping my sandshoes on in case the rocks were sharp. The undercurrent was powerful I could hardly stand, realising immediately that this was not going to be a smooth operation and would require at least two people.

Although I wasn't sure he understood, I thanked the old man profusely, and took my bearings, making sure that I could find this spot again. We returned to camp, and I soon realised I was unduly worried about the old man; he seemed to be fitter than any one of us.

I decided as a precaution to keep the location secret and not to move the camp closer to the exact spot. Instead, I would make the trip in the dingy every time purely in case we had uninvited guests. However, I had my doubts about finding anything at the wreck site as it seemed the currents were intense; I was sure that all the ship's contents would have moved by now. To me, this was evident as the story mentioned that when the shipwreck took place, all the passengers' belongings got washed ashore, and a century later, coins found on the beach.

Gold is weighty, and hopefully, some coins may have got caught up in the rocky reef, I prayed silently.

Thankfully, I thought that my years of experience diving for sinkers would come in handy. While in boarding school, I became a Catholic for the specific reason that they received a change to the daily stew on Fridays, fish and chips. Besides, Catholics did not have to wear a school uniform to church and were allowed to go in casual dress to early morning mass, leaving me ample time to go to the beach and dive for sinkers, which I sold back to the fishermen for pocket money.

Sarah and I were both of the same view: finding the wreck was wishful thinking but of great importance as money was desperately needed for us to get out of the country. As a bonus, the whole operation would enable us to be together on most weekends for a legitimate reason. In my mind, I already thought that we would have to overnight in the camp, and this provoked all sorts of pleasurable thoughts, and I began to anticipate the following weekend keenly.

After a lovely barbeque of sausages and steak, I offered the old man a cigarette; he eagerly took it and put it in his pocket. Realising that he probably hadn't had a cigarette in ages, I gave him the whole packet. Nobody seemed to call the old man by name; everyone addressed him as 'father' in Xhosa, and he recommended his grandson, as a watchman.

Mr Meth took the old man home while Sarah and I got the air tanks and whatever we thought needed to be checked over, ready to load on the pickup. Now that we had a trustworthy watchman who also lived nearby, I felt more confident with the security of the camp. His name was Vuzi, and he was 18 years old; he was also dreadfully fearful of his grandfather. Hopefully, this would encourage him to take his task seriously, and unquestionably the ten rands a week I promised him might also be of help.

Once Mr Meth returned, we rounded up the black youths, loaded all the gear that needed attention, and set off back to the trading store.

I asked, 'Do you genuinely think that your friend knows the location of where the ship, wrecked itself against the rocks? It was such a long time ago.'

Mr Meth replied, 'Well, if he is wrong, then nobody knows where to look. I have confidence in him. His forefathers were directly involved, and he told me that his grandfather showed his father and in turn, his father showed him the spot. They are relations of mine and are proud people. The only reason that he is willing to help is that I told him Sarah's predicament, and because of this, he and his family will help in any way they can.'

Leaving Sarah behind at the trading store was becoming more difficult to bear, and on my return to the hotel, I immediately went to the bar for a cold Castle lager and a chat with Clive for some company.

Clive was friendly but, on my entrance, a silence fell over the room, making me feel uneasy. Public bars in South Africa were for men only and supposed to only open for residents on Sundays. In small towns, the Sunday rule was not strictly applied, and they served non-residents as guests.

I was obviously no longer regarded as part of the community and wondered as to the reason behind this. Could it be that the locals did not like me taking over where the Germans left off or were it because of Sarah? Not wishing to offend anyone, I took my beer outside to enjoy on the veranda of the hotel.

Sitting all alone, I fingered out a cigarette from my packet of Mills. The inscription on the pack always amused me: 'England's luxury boardroom cigarette'. I bet you couldn't even buy them in England, but I liked them, and there is nothing better than a glass of Castle lager and a good cigarette.

I enjoyed the peacefulness of the large, empty veranda. My mind started wandering, trying to figure out how I got myself into this situation. After all, I came from a well-respected family and had what one would regard as an ordinary upbringing. My father was a medical doctor born in England who immigrated to South Africa to make his fortune. He married my mother, who is of Irish descent, but a true Afrikaner who refused to speak English.

I was brought up in Pietermaritzburg, South Africa and thought it was a normal childhood. Perhaps I was a bit unruly as my father gave me regular beatings for no apparent reason. Being the youngest, I mostly mixed with children older than myself and suffered a lot of bullying, learning bad habits early in life, causing me to challenge authority at an early age.

I had many problems at school, particularly with sport. Attending an Afrikaans school, it was compulsory to play rugby. I was keen to play soccer, but this was not available. I had to pursue this after school hours. The only way for me to miss rugby practice was to prove that I had joined a private soccer club and attended training three times a week to show that I was taking part in some sporting activity.

Not surprisingly, this marked me out as different as in Afrikaans' school's rugby was an absolute must. On top of this, I seemed to find schoolwork easy and, again, this made me stand out. All of this meant I found it challenging to fit in with the rest of the school children. Playing soccer also brought me into contact with more English-speaking children, and consequently, most of my friends were English, making it even harder to mix with my fellow schoolmates. The bullying continued throughout my junior school years.

At the age of twelve, I was moved to an English boarding school in East London, about six hours drive from my home in Pietermaritzburg. Making me feel cut off from my old life. However, by this time, the damage to me was done. Although not officially diagnosed, I must have suffered from some form of social anxiety disorder. I was constantly worrying about things that might never happen and lived with a fear that everyone was judging my every action, making it difficult for me to make friends or to trust anyone.

I did not know if the move to boarding school was supposed to be for my benefit or if was it a punishment for not fitting in. Academically I did well in this school, but being a border made me enormously unhappy, and I did all sorts of wayward things, like being caught smoking.

The local magistrate brought me back to the present with, 'Mind if I join you? You seem far away.'

Ronny Smith was a short, stocky man with a small moustache, perhaps in his fifties, and I found him a fair and kindly person. His daughter, Mary, worked in the telephone exchange and was well known to me.

Due to the age difference, I did not know him all too well, except for a friendly hello and the time I went to see him regarding the Germans' diving equipment. ' Certainly not, I was merely reminiscing and would be glad of the company.' I added that I had found most of the Germans diving equipment intact and that I had posted a guard to watch over the camp but had not done any diving yet.

'If I were younger, I would have been keen to join you. It sounds like it could be a great adventure. That is what I would like to discuss with you. You seem to have stirred up a hornets' nest with your friendship with Mr Meth's daughter, and now this diving for the long-lost *Grosvenor* treasure.'

I was a bit surprised as I did not think my friendship with Sarah was common knowledge. If the magistrate knew, everyone must be talking about it.

Mr Smith continued, 'I have predicted that something like this would happen. She is a beautiful girl and certainly whiter than most of us so-called white people. But the law is the law, and I feel that I must warn you that I am aware that the security police are interested in you. I think they are in admiration of her looks and would also like to get their hands on the treasure.'

The thought of the Security police brought shivers up my spine, all my youthful anxieties returning. These guys were the biggest bullies in the country.

'Clearly, my friendship with Sarah or hidden treasure is of no concern to the security police?' I enquired.

Mr Smith replied, 'There is no case that I can see to implicate the security police. That is why I think it is a personal matter. Be extremely careful; it is relatively simple for them to fabricate some trumped-up charges against you.'

I was dismayed, but thankful for his frankness and could only reply, 'What am I to do? I do love Sarah and would not like to give her up.' Mr Smith's advice was to get out of South Africa as this relationship could only end in disaster.

He explained further that although as a white man, I was not supposed to be in the Bantu homeland.

Everything outside the local villages on the Wild Coast was Bantu homeland, out of bounds to the white population, however, Being a local, this rule mostly ignored as several white residents have cottages on the coast. There are no racial segregation laws in the homelands, and if I see Sarah there, no offence is committed other than I am not supposed to be there.

He warned me that everything that happened in the village is subject to South African law and that we must be cautious.

He stated, 'If a member of the public reports you and the police lay charges against you. I will have to prosecute you even though I feel it may be unfair, and if in your shoes, I probably would also have fallen in love with Sarah, given half the chance.'

He also agreed to give me a permit allowing me to stay overnight on weekends when I went to search for the *Grosvenor* treasure.

Later that evening, as I lay on my bed, I tried to make sense of the weird situation we found ourselves. Take Sarah, for instance, brought up as a white girl in a boarding school in Lesotho where there is no racial discrimination. Still, on her return to South Africa, she immediately becomes a second-class citizen with no rights whatsoever.

What made it even harder to swallow, it was not the laws, but the mindset of the people; going by the reaction in the public bar, they looked down on me only because I was seeing Sarah.

It was difficult to imagine how Sarah must feel, born in a country that only accepted you as a second-class citizen. Having a white skin, not acknowledged by the black African people, yet at the same time, classified as non-white, you are legally not allowed to mix with or use white facilities.

It is as if this government is trying to force people like Sarah out of the country.

However, even if one had the money to leave, the government blocked this escape by enforcing currency restrictions on all would-be leavers, ensuring those who managed to escape these discriminatory laws would be penniless.

As far back as I can remember, I felt ill at ease living in South Africa and always had a yearning to go overseas, from where my dad's family originate. Away from this judgemental society. Perhaps, I was just too soft, the people around me seemed to have different values to me.

I never had the patriotic zeal that my friends appeared to possess, blindly and with great passion, supporting and obeying a government that I thought was corrupt.

I didn't think that I was a challenging sort of character, only that I could not understand things like spying and informing on one's fellow countrymen purely because someone in authority tells you to do it.

For instance, while working for the post office, I was asked to steam open a particular person's overseas mail, copy the contents and give this to the security police. This person was a religious minister, not a terrorist.

CHAPTER TEN

Mindful of my experience and the warning from Mr Smith, I knew that I had to tread carefully with the security police. They seemed to act as if they were all-powerful and untouchable; most of them were corrupt, thinking only of what personal financial benefit there was in each situation and then bending the law to achieve it.

Before the establishment of BOSS, the Bureau of State Security, the South African government looked at British Intelligence agencies for guidance in how to establish its security and intelligence agencies.

Some of the main aims of BOSS included identifying any threats to the country; collect, evaluate, correlate and interpret national security intelligence information. Another objective for the creation of BOSS was to coordinate the security activities of both the security branch of the police and the military intelligence division of the South African Defence Force (SADF). One of its primary purposes was also to coordinate intelligence work as well as to create a foreign espionage capacity.

The formation of the Z- Squad, also known as the Death Squad, was allegedly responsible for the killings that are issued by BOSS. The Z- Squad formed in the middle 1960s following an idea in which Security police began to eliminate ANC sympathisers inside townships preferably than taking part in the lengthy process of going through a trial. Allegedly the secret death squad was responsible for maintaining apartheid by carrying out a series of assassinations of political opponents, where these killings, made to look like accidents or suicide.

BOSS even got involved in the Angolan Civil War because it believed that Soviet Russia could infiltrate South Africa through Angola.

They seemed to get involved in all sorts of objectionable situations, a lot of these were not issues of state security but more political and sometimes even personal. They seem to act as if they were above the law. At the best of times, their motives were not to be trusted, and it is best to stay clear of them.

Pleased with myself that I thought to keep the location of the shipwreck secret. I now knew I had to be careful not to reveal exactly where we were going to dive as I was sure that the security police would take over the operation somehow by using legal powers the minute they knew where to look.

One of the security men who arrested the German divers used to be an ordinary policeman, by the name of Steve from Pietermaritzburg, known to be a bit of a bastard and of low moral standing, allegedly involved in blackmail and planting evidence.

The security police did not operate from the village. No one seemed to know where the local base was; always arriving as if from nowhere. I was hoping that this Steve was not one of the security Police covering our area, although they were all bad news.

People would joke that if you couldn't get a job, you join the army, and if they don't want you, you become a policeman. If you are an exceptionally substandard policeman, you join **BOSS** and become a security policeman. Whether this was the truth is debatable, the general opinion of the security police was exceedingly negative. Most people disliked them and avoided them, if possible.

I was brought up a God-fearing person with respect for the law, but the security police were an entirely different matter. As far as I could see, I was not a security risk to the country or involved in some terrorist plot. Therefore their interest must be for personal gain. Oh, how I loathe these sort of bullies, using their official status to try and make ordinary people feel degraded and humiliated. I wish that I could stand up to them.

All I was going to do was some diving, accompanied by a beautiful girl. I had permission to go diving from the magistrate and could not see how the security police could make any charges they could dream up, stick. If they were playing some game outside the law for their financial gain, I was ready for them and would attempt to fight back with everything trick I knew.

I do not know where I got this courage all of a sudden. Normally I would run a mile; I think Sarah had a lot to do with this, giving me the guts to stand up for myself.

The next morning, I went to work early to phone Sarah, keeping her up to date with developments, explaining to her that we had better not be seen together in the village and that she should not phone me, but instead that I would phone her.

It was safer as Lusikisiki had a manual exchange with operators, who could easily listen in to calls. I carried the keys to the post office, had access to the telephone exchange, and could make unrecorded calls after closing hours. Mostly I was missing her already and simply wanted to hear her voice. Disregarding the risk, we decided to meet that afternoon in the rectory, taking great care to remain unnoticed.

Next, I phoned Clive to see if he was in favour of swapping his pickup for my car permanently. My vehicle was of higher value and also more suitable for Clive to use in the seminary school where he would be studying to become a priest. Clive was more than happy with the arrangement.

Clive also commented that he hoped we found some of the treasure soon because if one relied on bar talk, my relationship with Sarah was heading for disaster and he thought that our arrest was on the cards.

I tried to explain to Clive that I loved Sarah, and it would be tough for me to stop our relationship at this stage. To this, Clive responded that if the police arrest us, that would be the immediate end of the relationship. Replacing the telephone receiver, I felt upset that he was not a bit more supportive. I was too dumb to take heed of his warning and simply carried on regardless.

During my lunch hour, I went to the general store and bought several small mirrors to give to Vuzi, our security guard, to use for signalling. I remembered that the Zulus used mirrors to signal each other in the bush when the police tried to raid their smallholdings where they grew cannabis amongst their maise crop.

After work, Sarah and I met in the rectory in the presence of Father Eric, to whom I explained everything, including the warning I got from the magistrate regarding the security police. He thought that we should proceed and also confirmed my reasoning that it could not be illegal to see Sarah in the rectory with him present. Father Eric warned us that the white residents would think we were up to no good, and there would be a lot of tongue wagging and that they would shun me.

Naturally, this was the least of my worries. All I could think of at that moment was spending the weekend camping with Sarah. Father Eric left the room for a few minutes, and we fell into each other's arms. Looking into her eyes, I could see her love for me, reinforcing my aspiration to see this through, regardless of the obstacles ahead.

The rest of the week I spent checking that all the equipment was ready for the upcoming weekend. I also took my newly acquired pickup to the local mechanic for a check-up to see that all was in good order. Chris, the mechanic, was a friendly local chap; his parents also owned a trading store in the area.

His garage was no more than a large corrugated shed suitable for working on one car at a time, but he knew motors inside out and gave the pickup a clean bill of health. He had also heard all the gossip going around and assured me of his support as he had known Sarah from a young age and agreed that she was a lovely girl.

It was strange that most people I spoke to personally were thrilled with the friendship between Sarah and myself. Still, when they were in a group, like in the public bar, they would preferably not include me in their conversation as if they were frightened to acknowledge me as a friend.

The week dragged on, and it seemed like ages for Saturday to arrive. I had taken the day off, wishing to make an early start. After checking that everything was loaded, I picked up Sarah, and we set off to the campsite where we were going to spend two whole days together without worrying who might see us. With total freedom, we could now behave like two ordinary young people. Sarah was as excited, giving me a beaming smile.

'You know I love you,' she proclaimed with a twinkle in her eyes. 'This new adventure makes me all excited, and I hope we find the lost treasure, but whatever happens, it will be great fun, especially that it is only the two of us together.'

I interrupted. 'We are not completely alone; remember there is Michael.'

Sarah replied, 'He doesn't count, he's my brother. Oh! What a nasty country, I do hope we succeed and can emigrate somewhere where we are all equal.'

'Slow down. Let's tackle one thing at a time,' I advised, touching Sarah's hand reassuringly.

'We will get through this. The most important thing at the moment is to be cautious and watch out for the security police, who I think are keen to collect whatever we find for themselves and will try to do this using any means possible.'

Sarah's father insisted that, for security reasons and that our relationship was not too obvious, we take Michael with us on each trip. I thought this would hinder all the dreams I had of any sexual activity with Sarah, but I agreed that it made sense.

We picked up our regular group of youngsters with Michael in the front and Sarah on the back of the pickup for part of the way. I tried to explain to them that we were not coming back the same day, but to them, it made no difference as they had family near the campsite. I told one of them to stay behind on this trip and tell the parents of those coming with me, that they will only be back on Sunday.

For the African kids, it was also a break, and they were indeed as excited. What a carefree existence they led, seemingly without a worry in the world. It suited me fine as there was always a need for extra help, even though it meant extra mouths to feed.

The trip to the camp was uneventful, except for the typical obstruction of livestock on the road and Sarah spotting several antelope. 'Oh, how beautiful!' she exclaimed as we passed a group of monkeys frolicking in the grass on the side of the road. The beauty and the overpowering sweet scent of the countryside were breath-taking, stirring hidden emotions in Sarah. 'This is truly a beautiful country, maybe, *just maybe*, one day there will be room for everyone.' From the corner of my eye, I could not help but notice the sad look on her face.

With my hand on her knee, I stressed, 'Oh, don't be sad, we are going to find this treasure. Have a fun time while searching and, when we find it, get out of this country. Maybe sometime in the future things will change and then we could come back.'

Sarah replied, 'Wouldn't that make a lovely dream? I don't think this country will ever change, let's get on with it.'

Conversation dried up as we approached the coast, with me concentrating on the tracks trying to be like a road, and Sarah afraid to say anything that would distract me.

CHAPTER ELEVEN

At the camp, everything looked undamaged thanks to the watchful eye of Vuzi, who I commended for doing such a good job. He informed me that some white people in a Land Rover came snooping. He thought they were police as they asked a lot of questions; they were in plainclothes.

I handed Vuzi the mirrors I bought, and we devised a code that he would use to signal if visitors arrived when we were out at sea. He immediately grasped the idea and knew what to do. I helped him to find the best position for his observation spot that also allowed an unobstructed lookout to the sea. Friendly signals would use one mirror, but if there were visitors, he would use two mirrors simultaneously.

To my delight, Sarah had organised all the unpacking and had the camp set up correctly. 'Well, this is nice; we might as well get the dingy in the water and do a bit of diving.'

Together with our young helpers we soon got the outboard motor fitted and fuelled. They were gently easing the craft into the water when Michael exclaimed, 'Look! 'Vuzi is signalling, using two mirrors.'

I could feel my heart beating a chaotic rhythm.

I was getting furious. I felt like screaming. Why can't we be left alone? We have committed no crime. Fundamentally, we have never even broken the immorality laws. The only time we made love was in the African homelands, where this law does not apply. Why do the police need to follow us? We are also not terrorist.

It was going to take all the inner strength I could muster to remain calm and try not to alert whoever was watching. I told Sarah and Michael to act naturally. Where I got the nerve from, I don't know. Perhaps it was Sarah's presence that gave me the confidence to remark.

'We will carry on with our dive, but purely as a precaution, we will only dive in the same spot as where we understand the Germans used to dive. We need to test the equipment, and it will be fun to confuse our onlookers. I am sure that it is the security police, they must have followed us from town.'

They must be incredibly keen, I thought. Although nervy, this is going to be a lot of fun deceiving them. I hope they are patient because I was in no hurry and entirely happy to enjoy diving and camping.

I started the outboard motor and guided the dingy through the river mouth and out to sea. It was only a short trip and barely beyond the breakers to the assumed spot where the Germans used to dive. The sea seemed relatively calm, with no visible rocks. I decided to save our air and use only snorkels while they watched. 'I do not think we need our wetsuits, but I will go in first to see how rocky it is down below. In the meantime, drop the anchor overboard, and I will give you a shout if it is safe.'

The dept was not alarming; I estimated about three metres extending to about fifteen metres, mostly sand with some rocky outcrops forming a reef. The sea was beautifully clear and warm. Coming up for air, I beckoned Sarah with a wave. 'Come on in, it's lovely, let's explore.'

Without hesitation, Sarah peeled off her tracksuit, revealing her lovely, slim body clad only in the smallest bikini you could imagine. I bet our observers were feverishly adjusting their binoculars. But, unfortunately for them, she swiftly joined me in the water.

There was an abundance of fish, such as mullet, feeding on the algae and zooplankton, with shrimp and prawns, in turn, providing food for predatory fish such as dusky cob and elf.

Coming up for air, Sarah remarked, 'I can't see how a treasure could be down here, the seabed seems to smooth. Maybe it is true that the Germans were spies and they simply pretended to be searching for treasure.'

I pointed out to her that the ship was made from wood and would have disintegrated a long time ago. All that would remain are metal objects buried under the sand or perhaps caught up in the rocks and, besides, this is the wrong place.

I added with a grin, 'I have already found the treasure I am looking for, and it's you. Let's enjoy the dive but watch out for sharks. Follow me to the rocky reef where we can search for creatures such as sea slugs. They have prominent forms and come in extraordinary colours. Let me know if you find any treasure. It would be fun to haul something up into the dingy to test the reaction of our onlookers. I am certain they are the security police.'

Sarah's body was breath-taking underwater, making me shiver all over knowing that we were going to spend that whole night together. What should have been the most enjoyable occasion of my life was spoiled by the security police watching our every move.

Reluctantly I turned my thoughts back to the job at hand and started searching for objects to put in our treasure net, hoping to excite the security police.

Sarah was right, I thought, the sand on the seabed was so smooth there was no even a beer can. After coming up for air, we moved even closer to the rocky reef. The sea life was now plentiful; I could also see the outline of a shark lurking nearby. Amazed that I was not frightened at all by the shark, it seems that it was only humans that frighten me. I gently held Sarah's hand to keep her calm and moved even closer to the rocks. It was now a lot shallower, and I could see rays of the bright sun penetrating through the water.

Amongst the rocks, I found some rusty metal objects, origin unknown, but suitable for my net; filling it to satisfaction, I tied it to the guide rope as it was reasonably weighty. We continued snorkelling for some time until it seemed that enough time had passed to satisfy our observers that we were looking for treasure.

Returning to the dingy, we made it seem as if hauling up our guide rope with the net full of scrap metal was of the utmost importance. Stowing the haul carefully on the dingy, we set off back to shore. I was not surprised to see the security police Land Rover waiting for us at the landing.

Jumping out to secure the dingy, I greeted them with the biggest smile I could gather; however, my insides were in turmoil. Trying not to shake, I put on a brave face. 'Hello, what are you guys doing out here?' I remarked innocently. As if I didn't know.

There were four of them; all of them had this vacant look in their eyes. I could tell there was not an ounce of compassion amongst the lot of them. These guys were sheep, used to only following instructions. If their boss ordered to jump into the fire, they would not hesitate. I don't think they knew the meaning of common sense.

The person responding was a short, plump man with small eyes and rubbery looking lips. I was sure that this was the same policeman I heard about in Pietermaritzburg, dismissed due to his alleged involvement in a fraud case. After that, he joined the security police.

'We heard you were diving for the *Grosvenor* treasure and wanted to make sure that you were aware that you must report all your findings to us,' he demanded.

'Oh! I did not know that the security police had an interest in what we find lying at the bottom of the ocean. I obtained permission to dive from the local magistrate, who told me that I should report any finds that I deemed to be of significant historical interest to him but whatever else I found would be a waste of his time.'

His face appeared flush, and I could see the anger in his small, slit-like eyes. 'We do not normally bother with people diving and looking for treasure, but in this instance, we are particularly interested in what you might find in your search.'

You could tell that these guys were born bullies, used to getting their way by using force. They weren't capable of solving a problem through discussion or mutual consent.

I knew that the only way to confront bullies, is to put on a brave face and stand your ground but because Sarah was involved, I had to be careful not to go too far as I did not know what these guys were capable of and I did not fancy 90 days in prison.

With a wide grin I replied, 'Well, I suppose we had better stop diving for treasure then until I have this legally sorted out with the magistrate and our local police. Because I can't see any future in diving here if you are sitting in your Land Rover watching our every move and I have to give everything I find to you to inspect. Why you might as well do the work yourself, or is it perhaps that you are scared of diving?'

I could see that he was genuinely getting angry now. In a shrill voice, he replied, 'I am the law out here and what I say goes!' With that, he jerked open the Land Rover door and beckoned to his mates to get in.

'What about what we found today, or are you now only interested in future finds?' I questioned with a cheerful smile.

Ignoring me and slamming the Land Rovers doors, they sped off into the distance. 'Well, that's that for today. I wonder what happens next. We might as well carry on and enjoy our weekend and hand in our finds to the local police station, purely to stir up matters more,' I explained to Sarah.

Unknown to me, I was treading on exceedingly thin ice. Truthfully, only because the local magistrate was involved did they tolerate my sarcasm.

While all this was going on, Sarah and Michael had a fire going and everything prepared for a barbeque. After a delightful meal we decided that if Vuzi could not spot the security police's Land Rover, we would go for an exploratory trip in the dingy to where the *Grosvenor* got wrecked.

They must have had enough for today as Vuzi gave us the all-clear signal. On arrival at the site, I noticed straight away that this was going to be a more challenging diving location as it was exceptionally rocky with strong currents making it difficult to keep the dingy steady. Today was a bright and calm day and the tide being also right. I wondered how many such days we would get in a year. Not many, I guessed.

'I believe we will need our wetsuits diving here for protection from the rocky reef,' I commented to Sarah.

'Michael will have to stay on the dingy, our little anchor will not hold against these currents,' Sarah answered with a worried look on her face.

Although it was about 400 meters from the shore, one could stand up on some of the rocky outcrops, but nearby the sea was dark, and it looked reasonably deep.

'I think if the coast is clear tomorrow morning, we will give it a go. You guys will have to remain in the dingy, and I will go down to investigate.'

Sarah protested 'I want to come down with you; I am sure Michael can look after the dingy on his own.'

' Certainly, but first, you will have to show him how to keep the dingy steady in one place while I investigate down below to make sure we have all that's required to do a proper search.'

Sarah seemed satisfied with that, and we headed back to shore. Vuzi was waiting for our arrival and told us he saw smoke in the distance and thought that it was the security police campsite. He laughed, stating that he would inform his granddad, who he was sure would instruct all his people to make life as difficult for them as possible.

I explained to Vuzi our plans for the next day's underwater descent, but for now, they could all go home, and we would see what happened in the morning. I also asked him to thank his grandfather in advance for any help he might offer.

Michael decided to go with Vuzi for the night, for the first time in what seemed like a long time, Sarah and I were alone together. I opened a bottle of white wine from the cooler box for Sarah and a cold lager beer for myself.

We contemplated the day's events sitting on our fold-up chairs, holding hands as we watched the sunset. It certainly was a busy day, and we had assuredly made some enemies; we decided that we would have to tread carefully from now on.

Soon the troubles of the day disappeared, and my thoughts turned to Sarah beside me. Her lovely body was clad only in a bikini and silhouetted in the fading light of the setting sun. An uncontrollable desire for her body was stirring inside me.

'Sarah, you know I love you. Every time I touch you, I feel excited.'

Sarah responded. 'I feel the same and can't wait to have you inside me; purely thinking of it makes me shudder all over. Come, let's make love now.' We entered the tent arm in arm and made passionate love until we both lay spent on our sleeping bags.

The next morning Vuzi and Michael were there early with a fire going, ready for coffee. I told Vuzi that he would again have to be our lookout as we were planning to dive in the correct spot that his grandfather showed us.

Vuzi agreed but stated that we should not have any problem this morning as his granddad's cattle somehow strayed into the camp of the security police and caused havoc, destroying their tents and somehow gave the Land Rover two punctured tyres. They must have radioed the local police station because the last he saw was that they had the two wheels loaded on a police van and were heading back to town, presumably to have the tyres fixed. Their camp now deserted.

The security police were at a bit of a disadvantage in the Bantu homelands as they had to do their job without upsetting the local tribes. Vuzi grandfather was the local chief in charge of this area.

It brought smiles to all; we enjoyed our coffee and breakfast in good spirits, and then readied ourselves for the day's adventure.

We soon had the dingy on the water, and with Sarah's assurance that Vuzi has signalled all clear of any onlookers, we made our way to the spot where the *Grosvenor* reportedly came to its end. This time I had my wetsuit on and breathed from an air tank as I was concerned about the conditions.

The sea was very choppy, and you could see the current swirling and running swells where the rocky reef started, exposing the rocks often. I decided that it was better to enter the sea some distance from the rocky area and then make my way underwater towards them.

While I descended to the seabed, Sarah remained on board, showing Michael how to control the dingy and keep it in the same spot. I made my way to where the sand meets the rocks where the ship allegedly was battered to pieces.

Barnacles, colourful sponges and all sorts of green algae covered the rocks. There were also many fish species everywhere. The current was powerful, and it was a task to concentrate on searching for objects but wedged in the rocks I found a strip of metal with what looked like a bolt protruding from one side. The piece of metal was old and severely corroded; with a lot of imagination, you could believe it was part of a ship.

With great excitement, I surfaced beside the dingy. 'Look, Sarah, I think we are on the right track!' I blurted, excitedly waving the corroded piece of metal.

Sarah grinned. 'That's only an old piece of metal; it could have come from anywhere.'

'I know, but I found it, and I have a good feeling that we are in the right place.' I don't know why, but I simply felt lucky and somehow knew that today would be the day.

After dumping the metal inside the dingy, I made my way back underwater. With renewed confidence, I started a vigorous search amongst the rocks. It was tough going as I struggled to keep the current from bashing me about, and under these conditions, I was surprised to spot more metal in the same spot but this time genuinely forced into a crevice between two rocks.

It now seemed that these metal objects were part of a barrel of some type, as they were curved. I continued to remove bits of metal from the crevice until I came upon a piece of metal, wedged into a rock inside the hole. I wiggled this metal object from side to side, trying to loosen it. To my amazement, the top of the stone came away; it was not underwater rock but a layer of metal encrusted with micro-organisms and covered by sea life.

Under this layer, I found a lot of round objects in the muddy bottom of the crevice. They were dark in colour, with yellow showing here and there. I started stuffing my net until it could hold no more. I returned to the dingy, pulling myself up with the guide rope.

In my excitement, I nearly threw my net in the dingy, remembering in time that Michael was on board. I did not want Michael to know of our finds as he was still young and vulnerable, and I knew that what we were doing would end up being illegal. I was not going to inform the authorities of this find.

Gesturing for Sarah to come closer, I whispered to her, 'I think I found it. Give me your net; I will tie mine to the side of the dingy. Try to keep calm; we don't want anyone to know. I am going down for some more.'

I managed to fill the second net, and then I wedged all the bits of metal back in the crevice and filled it up with loose rocks I found lying nearby. I tied a bit of cloth to the metal to mark the spot, making it possible for me to locate it again. Returning to the dingy, I tied the second net to its side.

I didn't know why, but I knew that we had to get away from this spot as I did not want anyone to know where we found the coins. We made our way back to where we were diving the day before. I asked Sarah to come with me while Michael managed the dingy.

The water was a lot calmer here and together we soon found a temporary hiding place for our treasure. Later that day after Michael had left with Vuzi, Sarah and I went back to retrieve the two nets.

Safely back in the tent, we started examining the find. To our amazement, with some rubbing to remove the dirt, the round objects began showing a gold colour. I washed a few of the coins with water and put one in my mouth to do a taste and smell test; there was no taste or smell at all.

'These are gold coins; we truly struck it lucky!' I exclaimed with delight. 'I am not going to report this. It is our ticket out of this hellhole of a country.'

I asked Sarah to take five or six coins at random and place them in her purse, the rest of the coins we packed in two hessian bags which I hid under the seat of the pickup.

It was sheer luck to have found these coins on our first dive. I thought that the security police would not expect results this soon, and because of this, we might get away with our stash.

'I am sure that these coins are gold but to be sure, and to know what purity of gold, I need some expert opinions. I can only get this in Pietermaritzburg where I have contacts in the jewellery business. If they are real, we will use the proceeds to leave the country and then get married. That is if you want to spend the rest of your life with me.'

'Oh, my goodness,' Sarah stammered. 'I have to tell my mum and dad. Where will we go? For sure, I want to be with you. There are too many things to think of.'

Taking her in my arms, I gently reassured her, 'I also have to tell my parents. Don't worry; we are not leaving tomorrow, it will be some time. What I want us to do is to keep dead quiet and continue to dive as if nothing has happened. In the meantime, I will take these coins to my parents' neighbour, Mr Cohen, in Pietermaritzburg. He has a jewellery shop, and their son Ted is a friend of mine. He works for his father as a trainee jeweller; they will help us to sell these coins.'

Father Eric had previously stated that if we left South Africa, he would also give us a letter from the church to the Home Office in England explaining our position and that the church would help us find accommodation and work.

I was secretly praying that this was true and that Mr Cohen would be able to help as the money we needed was far more than the individual annual allowance of cash one could legally take out of the country. Moreover, I didn't know if we were allowed to sell a treasure. Dealing in gold was not authorised without a licence.

Mindful of all these problems I thought that it would be sensible not to be greedy and only take a limited amount of treasure in case all went wrong. I could always come back at a later date to search for the rest.

I was excited with our find that my mind was all over the place, but sanity prevailed, and I called Michael to accompany us to dive where the Germans used to go. I wanted everyone to see that we were still searching underwater for treasure. I could see Michael was happy and proud to be given the responsibly of looking after the dingy. The sea was calm here, he was not truly needed, but it looked like we meant business.

Vuzi signalled that we had company, thus setting the stage precisely as I wanted it. We made as if we were searching underwater for a couple of hours and then Sarah and I returned to the dingy. Most of our diving was simply fooling around and enjoying the beautiful and abundant sea life.

We did not fill our nets with junk on this trip, and I was not surprised when there was no one waiting for us onshore as we arrived, but I was aware that our every move was monitored with binoculars.

We broke up camp and loaded all valuables on the pickup. Vuzi came back and told us that the security police had left. I instructed Vuzi to guard the campsite and asked him to be available the following weekend when we continued our search.

But first, I asked Vuzi to take me to his grandfather, the local chief as I wanted to thank him for helping to harass the security police. I had a carton of cigarettes with me, and I offered them to him as a gift. He was delighted, babbling away in Xhosa to fast for me to understand.

On the way back to camp, Vuzi explained to me that his grandfather was pleased with the cigarettes and that he will in future make life difficult for the security police, that they will wish that they were somewhere else and not in Pondo Land.

The young kids who accompanied us from town were also keenly waiting to climb on board the pickup for the return trip. They must have spent the weekend with Vuzi. It amazed me the freedom and carefree existence that the African people led without a worry in the world. When I picked them up, they did not question where we were going or for how long they would be away. They blindly came without informing their parents or anybody. I could only assume that this was the result of being brought up under this apartheid regime, where black people had to live from handouts from their white masters.

Returning to town, we first called at the rectory and showed Father Eric the two sacks of coins; they must have weighed about 5 kg each. He examined them and declared that they looked like the real thing. He was sure that the coins were pure gold as they were not corroded but only dirty; with a bit of rubbing, they soon cleaned up well. I told him we kept a few coins to show Sarah's parents and explained to him that I intended to take the coins to Mr Cohen to sell. With the proceeds, Sarah and I would move to England as our country of choice, seeing that I already had a British passport. Father Eric agreed and told us not to tell anyone who we intend to sell the coins to, not even Sarah's parents.

Father Eric explained it was fine to tell Sarah parents of our find but to protect Mr Cohen; we should not mention how we planned to dispose of them. He also acknowledged that we should tell

Sarah's parents that he would help with immigration and therefore he would need our passports, but that was all.

Father Eric thought that this would reassure Sarah's parents, his approval of what we had done. He also agreed that it was a good idea to carry on diving and searching for the treasure.

I told him about the security police and that I intended to hand the scrap metal we brought to shore to the local police. He laughed at this but warned us that the security police were an evil lot and that we should tread carefully. As there was no safe place at the hotel, I handed the coins to Father Eric for safekeeping until my trip to Pietermaritzburg. I felt great relief and could tell by Sarah's expression that she was also relieved.

Holding her hand, I remarked gently, 'I hope we have done the right thing; we are putting a lot of trust in Father Eric. It is our future.'

Sarah gave me one of her serious looks, saying, 'If we can't trust Father Eric, who else is there to trust? I have known him all my life, and he has never let me down.'

I left Sarah and Michael at the rectory to wait for me while I went to the police station to report my finds. Undoubtedly this was one of the pluckiest things that I have ever done.

At the police station, greeted by Sergeant Colin van der Merwe; he was a friendly sort of a guy, and we knew each other from the odd darts game in the local pub.

I swung the bag of scrap metal we salvaged on the first dive with great importance onto the counter and explained, 'Well, here is what I found diving at the *Grosvenor* wreck site this weekend.'

He looked at me with a bewildered look on his face, 'What do I want with your rubbish? The police station is not a tip, and we are not interested in what you find on your dives.'

I explained to him that the security police told me to declare everything I found to them, but as I didn't know where they operated from, I thought the correct thing was to hand everything into the police station.

Sergeant van der Merwe insisted that he knew of no law stating that I have to hand in everything I found at the bottom of the ocean, only that I must report any findings of value or historical objects to the local magistrate. He could not understand what interest the security police would have in what I might find on my dives. 'They must be mad, soon they will want us to report any fish caught.'

I laughed at this as I knew Sergeant van der Merwe to be a keen fisherman in his spare time. He told me to bin my findings in the nearest trash can and not to come and worry him again with such nonsense.

Sidetracked

CHAPTER TWELVE

Grinning, I returned to the pickup thinking that went well; now to explain everything to Sarah's parents and tell them of our plans. Returning to the rectory, I collected Sarah and Michael, and we set off to the trading store.

By appearance, you could speculate that Sarah's mother could be a descendant of the people stranded due to the wreck of the *Grosvenor* in 1782. Her features were European, although her complexion was a light brown, a consequence of sexual relationships amongst the local Bantu people and the stranded survivors of the ill-fated *Grosvenor*, which resulted in the establishment of a small coloured community.

These people of colour were not accepted by the black Africans or allowed to mix by law with the white community. They became outcasts from both societies and had to live in isolation. Treated as inferior, it did not surprise me that some women of colour had relationships with white men, mainly Europeans who were not yet brainwashed by the apartheid laws. It was therefore unsurprising that Sarah's mother had an affair with a visiting Swiss national and that Sarah was a result of this relationship. Although her mother was obviously of mixed blood, she was still a beautiful woman.

Sarah's stepfather was also coloured but was much darker in complexion and therefore more tolerated by the black community although still not entirely accepted by them. He did, however, do well in school and was good at bookkeeping. He became manager of the trading store owned by the local wholesaler.

He and Sarah's mother later bought the trading store from the wholesaler. Therefore, improving their income considerably. This increase in revenue allowed Sarah to attend a private school in Lesotho, where apartheid was not an issue.

It helped protect Sarah from bearing the full brunt of racial discrimination and made her feel that she was a human being. Only interrupted during school holidays on returning home, where Sarah had to stay in the confines of the trading store used only by black people. She could only go on the occasional visit to the town where her stepfather still helped the local wholesaler with the bookkeeping.

It made me wonder why these people would stick it out under such a foul and unfair regime. I supposed that they did not know any better and purely accepted their lot. The currency restrictions did not help, and after all, where would they go? The closest country is Lesotho, but there was no work and the government there only survived on foreign aid from other countries.

Mindful of all this, we set off to see Sarah's parents and break the news of our plans. Sarah was delighted with the idea of going overseas, marriage, and the whole concept of being treated as an equal. To her, this represented total freedom. Consequently, in her excitement, she jumped out of the pickup, ran to her mother, and blurted out everything in one gush.

'Slowly, slowly ...You are confusing and frightening your mother.' Her stepfather tried to calm Sarah's excitement. 'Let's start at the beginning. I gather you found some of the treasure. Come inside, and you can explain everything,' he smiled, leading us into the house.

Their house, situated behind the trading store was a comfortable three-bedroom bungalow. The sitting room was the central meeting place and was nicely furnished and decorated. Sarah took the lead, explaining to her mother that they found some gold coins and that I was going to give them to a friend to sell on our behalf.

Sarah father interrupted, 'You're sure it's gold?'

I explained, 'I have done the smell test by cleaning one coin and rubbing it between my fingers. I could not detect any smell at all. Father Eric also examined them and stated that they looked like gold pagoda coins.' Sarah presented Mr Meth with one of the coins; he was amazed and also thought that it looked like gold to him.

I continued, 'We are excited about this find, but I realise that without your help and that of your old friend, we would not have been lucky thus quickly. I know that I should thank him in person, but I am fearful of telling too many people about this, and therefore I ask of you to please thank him on our behalf after we have left the country.'

I asked Sarah to give me her passport as well as an old ring that I could use for her finger size.

'Why do you need all that?' Sarah inquired, giving me her serious look again.

Feeling full of happiness, I pointed out, 'We need plane tickets, and you will also need an engagement ring.'

Taking the coins in case the security police decide to search them, I left Sarah and her family in a state of excitement while I visited my boss, the postmaster, to ask if I could have Monday off.

Mr Visagie was a temporary postmaster and lived in a caravan behind the post office. The Department of Post and Telegraphs found it problematical to fill the position with someone of his rank permanently out here in the middle of nowhere. He came from the Orange Free State and was a conservative Afrikaans man in his fifties. We did not mix socially, and I did not get on well with him. His first response was a definite no. I explained to him that he had to see my parents on a personal matter of the utmost importance.

With a sneer, he remarked, 'I suppose you are going to tell them about your coloured girlfriend. I must also inform you that I have already reported your doings to Head Office and I am sure that they will be transferring you soon.'

Trying to control my temper, I replied, 'Sir, I came here to ask you kindly for a day off and did not expect insults and accusations. However, if that is your attitude, I will not ask but tell you that I am taking the day off and you can do what you want. I am not bothered.'

With that I returned to the hotel to find Clive because I wanted to use my car to go to Pietermaritzburg; I was scared there may be a lookout for the pickup as everyone now knew I was driving it. I certainly did not want to be stopped with all the coins in my possession.

After a change of clothing, I collected the coins from Father Eric and took the main road heading to Pietermaritzburg. The highway was gravel up to Kokstad and after that a well-maintained tarred road to Pietermaritzburg. Even though the gravel part of the journey was well maintained, one had to be careful because driving too fast might cause you to lose control of the vehicle. You had to be particularly careful when passing oncoming vehicles as the dust stirred up leaves you blinded for a few seconds. Even though these roads were fenced, they were broken in places allowing animals to wander onto the highway. When approaching villages, you had to be careful of pedestrians and dogs, especially on Sundays as there were a lot of drunken pedestrians.

Bearing this in mind, I held a leisurely but steady pace until I reached Kokstad and civilisation, then I was able to increase my speed and relax a bit. It was about a three-hour trip, and I had ample time to reflect on the reaction of my boss. As I mentioned before, the mentality of some South Africans astounded me. They were on a par with the Nazis during the Second World War, finding pleasure in reporting each other. Indeed, they must realise that something is wrong when a person with white skin gets classified as non-white.

Mr Visagie's reaction alarmed me, and I thought the sooner we could leave, the better as I could see trouble lurking on the horizon. With all these thoughts in my mind, the trip was soon over, thankfully without any incident or mishap.

I was relieved to be home again and greeted by surprised parents who were not expecting me to arrive unannounced. After an ice-cold beer, I told my parents the full story, also showing my mother a photo of Sarah and fetching the gold coins to show my father. They were both sympathetic and agreed that Sarah and I should leave South Africa as soon as possible. My mother, I could tell was sincerely concerned about my well being, but my father, I could not tell if he was just pleased to get rid of me.

Rising from my chair, I remarked, 'Well, I had better go next door and explain the situation to Mr Cohen and pray that he can help with the coins.'

My father also rose from his chair, saying, 'I will come with you if I may. It might put more emphasis on the importance of the problem.'

Next door, we were greeted by Ted, who showed us in to see his father in his study. I explained the situation and apologised for involving him in what might be an illegal transaction, but he was the only person I knew who might be able to help us.

With that I showed him a picture of Sarah and placed the coins on his desk for him to examine, adding that, to compound the problem, we would need the payment for the treasure in England as I had no way of smuggling money out of the country. Looking at Sarah's photo, Mr Cohen exclaimed, 'What a bonny looking girl! Do you say the government classified her as non-white? She sure looks white to me. It makes the mind boggle as to what this country is trying to achieve. I am glad you came to me for help; I will do anything in my power to assist you. We Jews know all about persecution. Now let me look at these coins.'

With that, he took a handful of coins and spread them out on his desk, examining them one by one and testing their hardness by biting into them. 'Well,' he stated, 'they certainly are gold, but I don't think they are pure gold. They seem to contain some alloy. Metals are mixed into the coins to make them more durable. These metals are usually silver and copper.'

After examining the coins for several more minutes, he continued, 'I would certainly be interested in purchasing all of them, but there's a problem. Firstly, I could only pay you the gold value as we would have to smelt them down and make them into jewellery. The second problem is that, at a glance, I would guess that they are worth way over £5000 and I only have £5000 in an English bank account.'

Somewhat surprised by the large amount he mentioned, I explained, 'In addition to money, I would also require plane tickets, an engagement ring for Sarah and it would be nice to keep two coins to wear on chains for remembrance. If I could achieve all this and £5000, I would be more than happy. Whatever profit is left would be yours for doing all this for us.'

Mr Cohen looked up with his magnifying eyepiece in place. 'Well, I will first have to examine and weigh each coin before I can make a decision. Can you come and see me in the store tomorrow at 10 am? It will take Ted and me all night to examine them and check their weight.'

We took our leave, escorted by Ted who whispered to me, 'You chose a nice girl to leave the country with, I wish it were me. Good luck. See you tomorrow.'

My father and I returned home. He assured me that Mr Cohen was an incredibly sincere man and would not cheat us. My mother was more interested in Sarah and wanted to know when she would be coming to visit.

I didn't think she understood how illegal it was for me to be going out with Sarah. Not wanting to alarm her, I merely confirmed, definitely before we go to England.

The following morning at 10 am sharp; I entered Mr Cohen and Ted's workshop at the back of the jewellery store. Mr Cohen was still busy examining some coins and Ted was busy buffing a few of them.

Mr Cohen greeted me. 'Come, sit down, and I will explain to you what we can do. Firstly, to put your mind at ease, I will be happy to do all that you mentioned last night. Also, I will write a letter to my brother in England who owns an upmarket clothing store, requesting him to find you some position in his enterprise and to help you find accommodation. I will give you an introduction letter.'

'That will be extremely helpful as I have never been to England and would not know where to start,' I explained thankfully.

'Now,' he stated, 'give Ted your friend's ring to help him select one of a similar size and do whatever alterations are required. I have decided to let you have a second-hand ring as the diamond would be of more value, and you could always sell or use it as security in case of need. Ted is also preparing two coins to wear on a chain. I think that is a nice touch.'

I handed Mr Cohen our passports as he had to arrange our plane tickets for thirty days from today, with a three-month return date. After he photocopied our passports, he handed them back with a cheque of £5000 drawn on an English bank. He also stated that if I had any problems cashing it, his brother would help us. He confirmed that he would also include it in the letter.

Ted showed me a ring he found that needed to be resised. I was very impressed; it was a large solitaire diamond and must be worth a fortune. 'Ted, Sarah would be delighted with that. It sure is a beauty!' I exclaimed with delight.

Ted promised that he would clean it up and make it look brand new. The two, coin necklaces and Sarah's ring would be ready in one week, and I should phone him to arrange collection. Thanking them again for all that they had done for me, I took my leave and headed back to Lusikisiki.

CHAPTER THIRTEEN

I went first to Mr Meth's trading store to explain everything to Sarah and her parents. To Sarah, the ring was of the most important, and I promised to collect it on Friday. 'Perhaps it is a good time for you to come with me to meet my parents. Please remember, the ring is a means to take money out of the country, and we may have to sell it in England.'

With an annoyed look, Sarah exclaimed, 'I will never sell it! It is the most important symbol in my life, and I will treasure it for as long as I live.'

I explained to Sarah's dad that Mr Cohen insisted that he is positive that his brother would employ both of us in his clothing store and would also help us to find accommodation. We would use his address on arrival for our immigration check. Together with all this and the letter from Father Eric, I could not foresee any problems.

Mr Meth suggested using his car if we were going to see my parents on Friday as this might help to confuse the police. I thanked him and agreed that it was a good idea; anything we could do to keep one step ahead of the security police would help.

Sarah's mother seemed a lot more relaxed and was helping Sarah look up addresses in England of family friends. I thought she was accepting me more now that our plans were coming together, and she was no longer worried that I would do a runner.

I told them what happened at work and asked them not to mention anything regarding our plans to anyone, especially not over the phone as I am sure their discussions would be listened to by the post office exchange staff. If the postmaster had already reported me to the head office, it would not surprise me if he informed the police about our doings.

Returning to the hotel, I again swapped car keys with Clive and thanked him for all his help. After a nice beer, I had a bath and decided to have an early night in preparation for what the postmaster might have in store for me at work the following day. I needed not to lose my cool and reveal the fact that we were leaving in thirty days. I had to keep in mind that what he did was of little importance.

The atmosphere at work was threatening, like a dark thundercloud. There was no play or joking amongst the staff, and all had stern faces. Mr Visagie threatened to have me transferred, and I told him he had no chance as he is only temporarily in charge and, anyway, who would head office find to replace me?

Nobody wants to come and work out here in the sticks.

Mr Visagie then threatened to deduct a day's pay from my salary. I told him if he did that, I would do my work so slowly he would need two people to clear up after me, and he would have to work overtime every day.

I was amazed at my ability to stand up for myself; it must be because I knew that I would be leaving the country soon.

After that, he ignored me for the rest of the day, but I knew he had it in for me and was waiting for an opportunity to strike back. Fortunately, I had an ace up my sleeve. Who would help in the telephone exchange in the evening? It was not in my job description, and I only did it as a favour. The extra income, however, was always welcome.

Five o'clock sharp I finished work and went straight to the pub, which was still empty, and had a beer with Clive. He told me that I was the main topic of conversation, but every time he approached someone to serve them, they would clam up, obviously thinking that he was part of the conspiracy.

Customers began to arrive. They ignored me and occupied the far end of the bar, keeping as far away from me as possible. I thought best to simply ignore the situation and asked Clive for another beer, which I took out to enjoy on the veranda.

I was barely getting into my beer when Mr Smith, the magistrate, and another gentleman approached and promptly sat down at my table. This gentleman, dressed in a dark suit, was about six feet five inches and built like a front-row rugby player.

Mr Smith introduced him as Mr Van Zyl from the Bureau of State Security. He didn't hesitate to come straight to the point. 'We need your help in supplying us with some information. I will explain the situation to you. The four German chaps we arrested were receiving arms from fishing trawlers on behalf of the banned ANC. They, not surprisingly, denied all of this and are unwilling to cooperate. As they are foreign nationals and we have no evidence, our hands are tied. All we can do is deport them back to their home country.

However, we know this took place. There must have been a go-between team collecting the goods and making payments, sort of a paymaster. We searched everywhere but could not find any cache of money or proof that these German chaps were on that team.

Now I have two avenues open to me to find out who their contacts were. I could arrest you and your coloured girlfriend and put an undercover team in to replace you, or you could try and get the information for me.

If you agree to do this, we will not disturb you and your girlfriend diving at the Mkweni river mouth. What's more, if you successfully find this information for me, I will help her to apply for reclassification as a white person.

Please remember that I cannot protect you in town that is in control of the South African police, and if someone reports you, they have to react and do their duty. Therefore please be careful.'

Not left with any options, but I knew to reclassify Sarah was something to be avoided as it would separate her from her family if successful. The chances of a successful outcome were exceedingly small if one goes by the methods they used to determine racial groups.

I replied tentatively, 'If I agree, what am I supposed to do?'

He smiled. 'There's nothing to it; I am sure someone will contact you asking a lot of questions. Get their contact details and pass it on to Mr Smith and we will do the rest. Also, if you find anything out of the ordinary give that to Mr Smith. We suspect that there is a large amount of money hidden somewhere, that they used to make payments.'

'Okay, I'll do it,' I replied, thinking that this would give us time. If I received any information, I would keep it to myself until the last moment before we left the country.

Still smiling, Mr Van Zyl continued, 'I will not tell my operators on the ground about our arrangement as it is best that they continue with their inquiries or the ANC will get suspicious, and they may not contact you at all. Rest assured, though, that my agreement stands and I will come to your rescue if something unexpected may happen. Mr Smith is my witness to that fact.'

Now, I understood why the security police were interested in my diving activities. They were not interested in the treasure at all but were looking for a large amount of money left by the Germans.

I finished my beer and made my excuses as I promised to meet Sarah at the rectory and was running late. Sarah was there waiting for me, and her lovely smile brightened up what was a tiring day.

I decided not to tell her what took place with Mr Van Zyl as I did not believe a word of what he promised. These people cannot be trusted; they all seem to work according to their self-made plans and would double-cross each other to achieve this, never mind betraying an outsider like me.

I explained to Sarah that I still had my job and that we must continue as usual diving for the treasure. I would try to get off work a bit earlier on Friday as we needed to return that same night from our trip to my parents, as not to arouse any suspicion. On Saturday, we would go to the Mkweni river mouth for the weekend and dive as usual.

Sarah had already explained to Father Eric our plans, and he agreed to put pen to paper to give us all the assistance the Catholic Church could muster on our arrival in England.

I had agreed to look after the telephone exchange that evening and told Sarah that I would phone her later. The telephone exchange in Lusikisiki was still an all manual affair consisting of two switchboards using the plug-in method; all calls channelled via the telephone exchange. Customers could not dial numbers, but instead, their phones had a little handle that you turned; this lit up the number on the exchange switchboard, allowing the switchboard operator to connect and obtain the required telephone number.

After closing time, only the police and the hotel offered an emergency connection to Kokstad, who provided a twenty-four-hour service.

The hotel would send my evening meal together with a couple of beers to the exchange. It was always quiet in the evenings, and I could phone everywhere in the country without any record or anyone listening to my conversation. First, I telephoned Ted and my parents to confirm that Sarah and I would be coming over on Friday evening to collect the tickets and her ring. I then had Sarah on the phone until I closed at eleven.

There were no street lights in the town, and you needed a torch to find your way home. That night even the hotel was in darkness, and I was relieved when I entered my room. Safely there, I poured myself a generous whisky and relaxed in my armchair, trying to put together all the pieces relating to what the security police were plotting and planning.

What was now evident to me is that I had them all wrong. The security police were not interested in the *Grosvenor* treasure but were after a more significant find. There seemed to be a more substantial and more crucial treasure hidden somewhere: the funds that the ANC or the German divers used to pay for the alleged arms drop.

That is why nobody seemed to state what they were looking for, merely, if you find something out of the ordinary, hand it over. They scoured the camp, yet, took nothing of value. Vuzi did tell me at the time that it was nobody from the local tribe.

I thought that the security police were stupid watching us search for the *Grosvenor* treasure as the chances of us finding that was remote. But the security police were after something else, and that is why they watched us closely.

It must be a large sum to get someone like Mr Van Zyl from the Bureau of State Security in Pretoria involved; he did not look like the ordinary security policemen, dressed in his dark suit.

I wondered what their next move would be without any inspiration. I made my decision, simply go with the flow and see what would happen as apparently someone should contact me. With that, I turned in for the night, thinking what an eventful day it had been; we certainly seemed to be in the spotlight, and we would have to watch our step.

The following day Mr Visagie asked if I could help every night that week in the telephone exchange. He was always friendly when my help was needed. I made a deal with him: I would work, providing I got two hours off on Friday afternoon and all of Saturday morning. It suited me fine as I thought it best if nobody saw Sarah and me together during the week, then, when we drove to my parents on Friday, it would be unexpected.

Fortunately, I also had the freedom of the exchange to make covert calls to whoever I wanted to and could chat to Sarah for hours and make all our preparations for the trip without anyone overhearing me.

That Thursday, while helping at the post office counter, I spotted a black face I recognised. It was Vuzi. Wondering what he was doing this far away from home, I called him to one side. The poor lad had come from Mkweni to give me a message. He told me that the people who used to meet the German guys were back; they searched the camp, asked all sorts of questions, and demanded to see me.

These were terrible people, he explained, and they have moved in at his grandfather's home, upsetting the whole family. He thought that they came from Johannesburg. In the mind of the local Africans, all bad people seemed to come from Johannesburg.

I explained to him that I could only come on Saturday and that these people would have to wait. I also gave him some money to catch a taxi back home and praised him for travelling such a distance. Well, I thought to myself, developments all around; it's going to be an exciting weekend.

Friday, I finished work at three and drove to Sarah's parents trading store, where I swapped the pickup for Mr Meth's car as arranged. I again had to ask Sarah to sit in the back until we were well out of the Lusikisiki area.

Sarah was a bit fidgety; I thought she was a bit nervous going to meet my parents. I tried to reassure her as best I could, stating that they already knew what she looked like and thought she was lovely.

The trip was uneventful, and, as I predicted, my mother loved Sarah. Being a bit over-attentive, I had to go next door on my own to collect the tickets and ring from Mr Cohen, who was disappointed not to meet Sarah.

I explained that my mother, taken with Sarah, didn't want her to leave. I invited them all over to my parents for a quick drink before we returned to Lusikisiki. The Cohens accompanied me back to my parents', and Ted even fetched a bottle of bubbly. After introducing Sarah and everyone was seated, I presented Sarah with her engagement ring. She was excited, not only kissing me but kissing everyone, with tears running down her cheeks.

I announced, 'Welcome to the family. How do you think Sarah Hammond sounds? '

Everyone raised their glasses to Sarah, who, teary-eyed, replied, 'This is the happiest moment of my life. The ring is beautiful, and Sarah Hammond sounds perfect as if it should always have been that way.'

We did not stay long as we still had to return to Lusikisiki that evening. Then we could go to the camp at the Mkweni river mouth early the next morning. I had not yet told Sarah about Vuzi's visit and his information about the bad men.

Sarah's ring had some hypnotic powers as she must have stared at it all the way home. I explained to her that she should not wear it in public as our relationship was illegal and people would wonder where the money had come from to pay for such a ring.

Sarah shrugged. 'Tonight, I will wear it all night; besides, I will wear it every night until we get to England. It is the most beautiful ring in the whole world, and I love you the most in the world.'

It was an uneventful trip back. Putting care to one side, I did not have the heart to tell Sarah to get in the back of the car as we neared town. Fortunately, nothing happened, and we arrived safely at Sarah's parents', with Sarah still admiring her ring.

Sarah's mother was also very impressed with the ring. I made a point of showing her the plane tickets as I knew she did not fully trust white men, and I hoped that this would put her mind at rest. Until now, I had not even shown Sarah the tickets, and this created even more excitement. I also gave her the two coins with their new gold chains to keep in a safe place.

I showed Mr Meth the letters and the cheque from Mr Cohen. He was enormously impressed and wished us all the best.

Sarah told her mother that as soon as we settled, they should all move to England. Mrs Meth explained that would be impossible as they had the store, but it might be a good idea for Michael to emigrate when he was a bit older.

I asked Sarah to keep everything in a safe place, together with her letter from Father Eric as I did not trust my hotel room; anybody could enter it during the day to search my belongings.

Nobody needed to realise that we had found anything or that we were going away. I wanted everything to continue as if nothing had happened until the very last moment. Mr Meth agreed and advised that we should not even tell Michael, who was already asleep. I kissed Sarah goodnight and arranged to pick her and Michael up at nine the next morning.

Driving back to the hotel, I felt excited enough to scream. 'We had achieved the impossible dream. Finding the gold coins and even having tickets for our flight to England.'

Deep inside me was this nagging doubt. Do not get excited; we are not there yet. Close, but not there. It is essential to keep our cool until we board the plane. One wrong move now will jeopardise all our achievements.

With all these thoughts mulling in my mind, I struggled to go to sleep that night.

CHAPTER FOURTEEN

We headed to the camp at the Mkweni river mouth on Saturday morning, with Michael next to me in the cab and Sarah in the back. Once the town was well behind us, I asked Michael to swap places with Sarah as I wanted to speak to her.

I could tell from Sarah's expression she was getting fed up sitting in the back and wanted to be in her rightful place, beside me. I asked her to be patient as there were only four weeks to go and that we should not rock the boat now. I also informed her about Vuzi's visit and the so-called bad men. We both agreed not to tell Michael and that I would handle these men while she tried to distract him.

Every trip to the wild coast was an adventure, the abundance of wildlife, made it difficult to concentrate on your driving, there was much to see.

Stubborn cattle with hundreds of acres for grazing grassland, monopolised the gravel road as if to compete with the traffic and refuse to get out of the way.

It is no good blowing the pickup horn. The cattle simply stare at you with there big brown eyes. Several times, I had to get out, smack then on the rump to chase them off the road.

I turned to Sarah. 'You must admit this is a beautiful country. I think the time will come when we are going to miss, all of this beauty.'

Sarah answered. 'It is a pity about the people and their laws.'

On arrival at the camp, everything seemed reasonable with Vuzi there looking after the equipment. He told us that the security police were there several times during the week and had a good look around the camp. There presence keeping away the bad men, who also wanted to look through the campsite. They desperately wanted to see me, and I should accompany him to his grandfather's place.

I asked Sarah and Michael to get the dingy ready for us to go diving on my return.

Vuzi guided me, negotiating the pickup across grassy fields until we reached the complex where his grandfather lived. His home consisted of six, round huts, beautifully painted white and decorated with red terracotta, all enclosed by a six-foot wattle fence. We entered one of these huts, where Vuzi introduced me to two black men. They were not from the rural Pondo tribe as they both wore suits and had a menacing look about them.

Vuzi left us, and one guy, who I assumed was the leader, introduced himself to me as Mr Mthetwa and a member of the ANC. They both bombarded me with questions, and it felt like a second interrogation by the security police. What it all boiled down to was two points: had I found anything of value and was I going to replace the four German guys they had dealt with before?

The first thing that came to mind was that this was evidence beyond any doubt that the four German divers were definitely up to no good; indeed, they were mercenaries helping the ANC.

I explained to them that I did not know what the German guys were doing. Sarah and I were searching for the *Grosvenor* treasure. I also explained to them that we had not found any treasure yet, and we could not understand what this treasure had to do with the ANC.

After mumbling a few words to each other, the leader again addressed me, stating that the local chief assured that I was trustworthy and therefore, they were willing to confide in me. Mainly, I think they had no choice.

It seemed that they had entrusted large sums of money to the Germans to use as payment for certain goods. With the Germans arrested, no more articles would be delivered, and they had no idea how to retrieve their money.

I explained to them that I had no knowledge of any money and that the security police had searched the camp several times and found nothing. Now I understood why the security police were interested in me.

'The reason the security police cannot find anything is that they don't know what to look for,' he stated. He continued to explain that instead of cash, they used diamonds for payment, and the German guys must have hidden them somewhere. He then gave me his card with a Johannesburg phone number, stating that if I found their stones to please contact them and that I would be well rewarded. The name on the card was Mr Zaba Mthetwa.

Although I had no interest in the reward as I felt that these guys could not be trusted, I asked, 'How much would the reward be if I happened to find your diamonds?'

Mr Mthetwa replied, 'We will pay you £50,000 sterling into any bank account, anywhere in the world.'

The reward was impressive, making me wonder how much the diamonds were worth in total. Making it was a serious incentive to search for them, although I doubted if payment of such a reward was ever on the cards.

I explained to them that I had no idea as to where to start looking for these diamonds and thought it was a hopeless task, seeing that the security police had searched the camp several times. However, if I happen to find something, I would call them straight away.

I returned to our camp with Vuzi, thinking to myself that phoning them would be the last thing I would ever do. Finders Keepers.

I asked Vuzi where the German guys used to do most of their diving, purely to confirm that we were in the right place. I knew that the young Africans would have observed the German divers meticulously and that they would have been the main topic of conversation in the evening around the campfire. Vuzi stated that it was always in the same place, directly in front of the camp.

The Wild Coast is renowned for its big waves and rough sea, creating reasonably strenuous diving conditions, scuba diving is not particularly popular, this region is suitable only for experienced divers.

However, directly in front of our camp was a bay, and the water was reasonably calm. Still, the river inflow next to the campsite created poor visibility underwater, usually in the region of 3m with a maximum of 12 or 15m in ideal conditions.

The Wild Coast lies in a summer rainfall region and, as many rivers flow into the ocean here, winter is the best time to dive.

Sea temperatures usually exceed 17C and can go as high as 23C when the warm Agulhas Current flows close to shore. The water is cleaned by the offshore south-westerly winds, which also flatten it to a degree, while the north-easter brings cold, dirty and choppy seas.

The germans always stuck to diving in front of the camp where the conditions were relatively calm and pleasant. Confirming to me that their motive for treasure diving was not honourable and they were in reality, smuggling arms as the security police alledged.

At the camp, Sarah and Michael had the dingy ready to go. I sent Vuzi on his mirror duties; he signalled the presence of the security police as soon as we set off. After about an hour of searching underwater, and mostly simply enjoying ourselves, we returned to camp with only some more scrap metal for a laugh, to keep the security police captivated.

While Sarah and Michael prepared the barbeque, I made a great show of examining the scrap metal, but secretly studied the camp for any sign or marker to indicate the hiding place of the diamonds. I took my fishing rod as camouflage and explored the shore of the river where we land the dingy. Searching everywhere, even amongst the rocks but still could not spot anything that could be a pointer or a clue as to where something was hidden and decided that since the security police could not find anything either, the diamonds must be buried in the sea somewhere.

That afternoon and the following morning, I made an extensive search of the seabed and rocks in the same place where the Germans used to dive, but without any success. On Sunday, the security police came to see what we had found. They were dreadfully rude as usual and not impressed with what I showed them; after poking through the scrap metal, they charged off in their Land Rover.

I could not understand their aggressive attitude. For sure the Security Police must realise that by being a bit more friendly, they would achieve more. Even if a cold beer is there only reward. I know, and they know that if I find the diamonds they are looking for, I would never in a million years give the jewels to them, while they are aggressive towards us. It can't be solely because of Sarah's presence. We were for all intents of purpose in another country as the South African laws don't apply in the African Homelands.

Later Vuzi explained to me their anger. A group of cattle found their Land Rover offensive and had bored holes into the bodywork in several places. This group of livestock also destroyed their campsite.

After that, we rounded up the African kids and went home. I felt somewhat disappointed after our lucky experience the previous weekend; now this weekend, nothing. The following weekend, it was the same. Even though we did a thorough search, we found nothing. I was getting worried as time was running short. We had only two weeks left, which meant that next weekend would be our last attempt to search for the hidden diamonds.

I had not yet told Sarah that it was diamonds that we were looking for, only that some money was hidden somewhere by the German divers. The people involved looked nasty, and I did not want to get her or her family involved.

The whole week my thoughts were on those diamonds, trying to figure out there hiding place and where I would hide something like that.

I concluded that it would not be safe to hide it in or near the campsite as there were too many African kids messing around in the area.

It had to be in the sea and in relatively deep water, where no one will find them by chance. After careful consideration, I decided that if I wanted to hide something on the seabed, I would tie a float of some sort to a fishing line or cable attached to an anchor. Come to think of it; they must have had some marker to show them where to dive.

Finding the coins was sheer luck, as I put no thought at all into where to search. This puzzle, however, was going to require brain work, although I thought a bit of luck would also come in handy.

On Saturday, we set off to the camp and prepared to dive for the treasure again, while I secretly searched for the hidden diamonds. I still questioned Vuzi as to the exact location where the Germans used to submerge. It seemed we were in the correct area.

I decided to spend more time searching the surface for anything floating. Asking Sarah and Michael to help without explaining to them that we were searching for diamonds, only that the Germans must have left some marker where they used to dive and that I would like to find the exact spot.

Vuzi signalled that the security police were there again, watching our every move. I was disappointed, as I thought that they had given up on us as they were harassed by cattle every time they spied on us. Their presence made it difficult to search on the surface for some kind of float, forcing us to resume diving. I did not want them to think we were looking for anything other than the treasure.

That evening we sat around the fire. I had brought my guitar and played some popular melodies, accompanied by Sarah singing in her magical voice. God, I thought, I genuinely care for this girl. How could the government classify her as non-white? The sooner we get out of this miserable country, the better. Listening to Sarah, I thought what a delightful talent she has. When we get to England, I will encourage her to develop it.

The next morning Sarah and I set off early. Michael was still asleep, and we decided on this early start as I was keen to do a thorough search to find the marker left by the German divers. After searching for several hours, Sarah shouted, 'What is that floating in the water?'

I steered the dingy towards the object, and there it was, a dirty blue fisherman's float, the sort that you would typically find on nets. It was in clear sight but exceptionally difficult to spot due to its colour. Not knowing what we were looking for, we must have passed it several times.

I asked Sarah to hold the dinghy steady while I followed the float's guide rope to the rocks below. They secured it to a piece of metal wedged in between the boulders. Having found the area I needed to search, I resurfaced for some air and fitted the tanks to give me the time to make a more thorough search.

I avoided the rocks where they anchored the float and moved to a nearby group of rocks, thinking that nobody would hide something in such a prominent place. My luck held and sure enough, there was a small tin, recently wedged between the rocks. I knew immediately that this was it; the tin was still clean, with no traces of corrosion or any sea life encrustations.

I surfaced next to the dingy and handed the tin to Sarah while I undid my air tank and fins. Sarah struggled to open the tin and gave it back to me. Using my pocket knife, I managed to prise open the lid.

'Oh my God!' Sarah exclaimed. 'What are those stones?'

'These are uncut diamonds. And that is what everyone has been looking for, and we better hide them before someone spots us with them. Try and hide the tin in your clothing until we get to the camp.'

Getting back to camp, Michael was still asleep, and Vuzi had scarcely arrived back, ready to proceed to his observation post. I hid the tin of uncut diamonds under the seat springs of the pickup and asked Sarah to act ordinary and make as if we are getting ready to go diving for the day.

After waking Michael, we loaded the dingy and Vuzi signalled the all-clear; we set off back to the usual diving spot. On our arrival, we got a signal from Vuzi that the security police had returned.

It seemed that our early morning trip went undetected; I told Sarah we should merely enjoy the dive for a couple of hours as today would be our last day.

While floating about after coming up for air and while out of earshot, I explained to Sarah that she should not tell anyone about the diamonds, not even her mother as this could be incredibly dangerous to her entire family. Some people would kill for these stones as they are worth a large sum of money. To top it all off, it was also illegal to possess or deal in uncut diamonds, and we would have to smuggle them out of the country.

After about two hours of seemingly exploring the area, which in reality was simply messing about, I thought that we had put on a good enough show for our observers. Sarah and I climbed on the dingy and told Michael to take us back to camp.

Who should be waiting for us as we reached the shore? It was our friends, the security police, and they were not in a friendly mood.

'What have you found today?' The fat, rubber-lipped leader demanded. I explained to them that we had found nothing and that it was a wasted morning.

'I don't believe you. We are going to search everything,' the leader barked at me.

'You're welcome. But why are you this suspicious today?' I replied, giving him the most innocent look, I could produce. I was wondering at the same time if they thought that the public would help them when they displayed this kind of attitude.

'Never mind, we know everything.'

With that, he told his mate to search the dingy and the camp. As we were dressed only in our swimming costumes and were not concealing anything, he did not attempt to examine us.

After a thorough search of the dingy, he turned to the camp and the pickup. My heart must have stopped beating at this stage, but to my delight, he found nothing. He must have searched half-heartedly, I thought, he was more interested in the dingy. After a few more insults and warnings that they were going to get us, they climbed into their Land Rover and drove away.

What bullies, I thought. As my heart rate returned to normal, I turned to Sarah and complained, 'I think I aged another ten years. Oh, I do hate these people. Let's have something to eat and get out of this place.'

We had a light meal, and I had a cold beer to steady my nerves, after which we packed up our gear, leaving behind the diving equipment, not to give away the fact that we were not coming back.

After dropping off Sarah and Michael at the trading store, where I bought a packet of putty and returned to the hotel, ordered a beer and went to my room. Locking the door securely, I opened the tin of uncut diamonds onto a sheet of paper on my bed and wedged them one by one into the putty, which I divided into three sections. One section fit inside my camera and the other two parts each fit into old spectacle cases I had leftover from my sunglasses and reading glasses.

I had seen diamonds smuggled in this manner in some movie and thought I would try the same trick. I made this into two parcels, one containing the camera and a spectacle case along with some old clothing addressed to me care of Mr Cohen's brother in England. The second parcel contained the remaining spectacle case and some more old clothing; I sent this parcel to Sarah, also care of Mr Cohen's brother.

I was carrying the two parcels wrapped under my raincoat in a way that was not conspicuous. I walked to the post office, across the field, hoping that no one would see me. After checking to see that the postmaster was not around, I sneaked into the post office using my key.

Once inside, I completed a customs declaration for each parcel, affixing the necessary postage and placed them in a nearly full postbag and sealed it, ready for despatch the following morning.

I sneaked back to the hotel the same way I came, ordered another beer and, to avoid bar talk, I took my beer to the veranda where I relaxed and lit a cigarette, allowing all the tension to drain from me. I tried to concentrate only on the thought that next Sunday we would be on a plane en route to England.

This last week Sarah and I will have to be extra careful. Being caught together now and arrested would shatter all our carefully laid out plans, especially now that the end of this forbidden way of life was near.

Therefore, we had purposely not made any arrangements to meet, for safety sake. I was again helping out in the exchange that Monday evening. Allowing us ample time to discuss our plans for the weekend privately.

I was first at work on Monday morning. I wanted to get the mail ready for despatch before anyone noticed the sealed parcel bag. It was part of my duties, but you never know, someone might purely offer to help, and I did not want to explain to all.

I was unduly worried; nobody took any notice or offered any help. It was a lousy part of the job anyway.

That evening I told Sarah that the diamonds were gone. We also decided not to see each other until I picked her up on Friday after work on the way to my parents. Because I worked evenings in the exchange, I got the Saturday morning off, as if that mattered now.

The week dragged on, and it seemed a long time before Friday arrived, feeling fed up with the post office at that time. I did get one thing sorted out; we transferred the pickup to my name and my car into Clive's name.

Having confided in Clive that we were leaving on Sunday, I handed him the card given to me by the ANC guy and explained to Clive what the state security officer wanted me to do.

I told him that he did not have to do anything; he could tear up the card if he wished. The decision was up to him if he decided to contact the magistrate, please wait until Monday to give us time to get out of the country.

Clive grinned. 'I am happy for you guys. I have overheard a conversation between the owners of the hotel. They are about to ask you to leave as your stay here is causing friction amongst the guests. There was also a discussion in the bar about arresting you, but Sergeant Van Der Merwe stated to do that someone had to make a formal complaint and be willing to testify to that in court. It seems that at this stage, nobody is coming forward.

It is good that you are leaving as I would say that your position here is becoming untenable and that someone is bound to make a complaint to the police very soon.'

It seemed as if we were leaving in the nick of time, and hopefully, our luck would hold out until Monday when we would safely be in England.

CHAPTER FIFTEEN

Eventually, the time to leave arrived. I loaded my suitcase and few belongings into the pickup without being observed and set off to the trading store to pick up Sarah. She was ready and waiting; her nerves also frayed. After loading her suitcase and difficult farewells to her family, we set off. Fortunately, by this time it was getting dark, allowing Sarah to sit in front with me. However, I told her to keep her head down until we were some distance out of town. After that, I did not worry as few people would realise she was coloured.

The three-hour trip to my parents went without any incident, and Sarah and I were relieved to arrive. Our nerves badly tattered from this cloak-and-dagger existence. We could not wait to be on the plane and out of this mess.

My parents were excited to see us, with my mother taking complete charge of Sarah, pampering her as if she were a little girl. Being stuck with sons, I think she had always secretly yearned for a daughter.

After a lovely meal, we retired to the lounge, and I shared one of my dad's finest cigars. I explained to him about the pickup, suggesting that he could sell it if it is of no use to him. He was pleased, saying that the truck would come in handy as he always had problems finding a vehicle for removing garden waste and going fishing.

I noticed Sarah was wearing her diamond ring and her chain with the gold coin. I thought that I should caution her but decided what the heck; she was enjoying herself.

The next day I went to visit Ted and Mr Cohen at their jewellery shop to thank them again. The prime reason, however, was that I did not know what to do with myself. Sarah and my mother were involved in doing each other's hair and deciding what to wear. I felt that I was getting in their way.

I was proud of my mother; there was not a thought in her head about Sarah being non-white. She had even prepared a double room for us. I had to remind her to put us in two separate rooms purely in case we were raided by the police as there was a prison sentence for knowingly allowing the use of premises for interracial sex.

Merely sleeping in the same room was sufficient evidence to prove interracial sex, and this offence would carry a penalty of up to five years' imprisonment.

My parents were driving us to the airport in Johannesburg to see us off, making it a significant occasion for them. They were planning to spend the night in a hotel at the airport as our flights were at 8 pm.

We set off at 10 am as it was about a six-hour drive to Johannesburg. Again, I had to correct my mother as she promptly got in the front seat with my father. I explained to her it was safer if I sat in the front, and she accompanied Sarah in the back.

I thought that if I don't relax more, I will end us suffering from some traumatic stress disorder

I felt that if my mother were involved in an illicit relationship, the police would arrest her within the first few days. You could not blame her as Sarah was white, you had to think twice before you accepted she was coloured. In effect, at all our stops for refreshments, Sarah used the white facilities and was not questioned once.

We arrived at Jan Smuts Airport slightly after 5 pm, expressed our goodbyes to my parents, changed our currency to pounds, checked in with BOAC, and proceeded to the international lounge.

I hugged Sarah and exclaimed, 'We have now left South Africa! There is no apartheid in here, and we can do what we like'.

From that point onward, our hands glued together as we wandered all over the international lounge, savouring the freedom of being able to behave like two ordinary people in love. Eventually, Sarah got tired of walking about, and we settled near the bar with a glass of wine each, waiting for our flights. We were both excited as this was our first time to experience flying on an international airline; we were unaccustomed to the procedure and found everything fascinating.

Soon the flight was called, and we had to proceed to the boarding gate. The stewardess checked our boarding passes and directed us to our seats. Sarah was impressed with the flight stewardess and her routine safety instructions. We secured our safety belts and tried to anticipate the moment the plane left the tarmac, and we were in flight.

The take-off was very smooth, and soon we were allowed to remove our safety belts and have a cigarette. The first and only stop was Nairobi, where the aircraft refuelled. I was amazed at how busy they kept us during the flight. I had no sooner finished my cigarette then the flight hostess was coming around with the evening meal and wine.

After the evening meal, I ordered a whisky for myself and a glass of wine for Sarah. Now, I thought, we can relax a bit and cuddle up together under the blankets provided by the airline. But no, a movie had started and Sarah, who had never been to a cinema or seen a television, was excited, and we simply had to watch. It was a Clint Eastwood film, *The Good, the Bad and the Ugly.*

The film finished as we landed in Nairobi, where some passengers disembarked, and a few new passengers boarded. We went through the same procedure on take-off; Sarah and I felt bored with it all as we were now old hands at flying. This leg of the journey was a bit more peaceful, and soon Sarah and I were huddled under our blankets, fast asleep.

The next morning, we arrived at Heathrow Airport, where I told the immigration officer that we wanted to claim asylum. He called his supervisor and led us to an interview room where I showed them the letter from Father Eric and Mr Cohen, telling them the full story.

The lady conducting the interview left us alone in the interview room, presumably to make some phone calls to verify our story and to discuss the case with her senior officer. Then Sarah and I were separated. The same lady questioned me as to why we wanted to claim asylum. Admittedly, we could enter England as tourists and get married? As I had a British passport, they would then automatically grant Sarah leave to remain in the UK as my wife.

I frowned, explaining, 'I do love Sarah and I do want to marry her. I am a bit scared that if she has no choice in the matter and had to marry me to get residence in England, she might resent me later on. I would much prefer if you grant Sarah permission to remain in England as a single person and then if she still wants to, we can get married in six months. Then it will be her decision, made of her own free will, with no threat of deportation hanging over her. However, if this is not possible, I would be happy to marry her straight away and hope for the best.'

The lady interviewer seemed a kind person, smiled, and promised that she would see what she could do to help us. I was then left alone for an extended period and eventually called to join Sarah, where a smiling lady handed us our passports. Sarah's passport had a big stamp saying 'Leave granted to remain in the UK for an indefinite period', giving her permission to take up employment or to start a business. She received a letter to confirm this.

Leaving the immigration area, I exclaimed, 'Welcome to England! I am glad that is over, I hope it was not too much of an ordeal for you.'

Clinging to my arm, Sarah announced, 'They were very friendly; all the waiting made me anxious though. I think it was the letters from Father Eric and Mr Cohen that did it. Did you know Mr Cohen's brother is a big shot in the Jewish community here?

The Jewish and the Catholic Church were ready to send their representatives to plead the case on our behalf. Confirming that they would find us accommodation and employment, guaranteeing that we would not be a financial burden to the UK. Then after five years, I can apply for British citizenship. Oh, James, I'm delighted. Let's first have a cup of tea before we do anything!'

After collecting our luggage and clearing custom, we entered the arrival hall, which was full of people waiting for passengers. I was dumbstruck by the number of people and did not know which way to turn until Sarah grabbed my arm and called out, 'Someone is holding a board with your name on it.'

It turned out to be Mr Cohen's brother, who enquired, 'I hope you had a good trip and that immigration was not too much of an ordeal?'

'The trip was fine, and the immigration people were extremely nice. It simply took such a long time. But all is well now, and Sarah has permanent residence.'

Mr Cohen nodded his head, saying, 'I am pleased. I have booked a room for the two of you at the Russell Hotel for a couple of days, to adjust and get over your jet lag before we consider something a bit more permanent. Do you have enough cash, or would you like me to cash the cheque my brother gave you?'

I replied, 'Thank you, we have enough to see us through for a few days, then we will need to cash that cheque and put the proceeds in a bank account for safety.'

Leading the way, Mr Cohen declared, 'I will drop you off at your hotel and then tomorrow my driver will pick you up at 11 am, and we can go to the bank I have used for years to open an account. I know the manager personally, and there should be no problems. At the same time, I will show you my clothing store, where I hope you will work once you have settled.'

Sarah had never been in a hotel before and fell in love with the magnificent Victorian architecture of the splendid old building. It had been lovingly restored and still retained its original grandeur inside and out. She continuously commented on everything. 'James, look how lovely and clean everything is.'

As we entered our room, Sarah cried out, 'Look, it has a TV! What a lovely bed and we have a bathroom. Oh, what luxury! James, pinch me, I need to wake up, this must be a dream. I can't explain how happy I am. Thank you, James!' Sarah marvelled, throwing her arms around me.

After a shower and a change of clothes, we went downstairs to the bar and restaurant, where we had a round of sandwiches as we missed lunch. I ordered a beer; it seemed stale and served warm, not what I am used to at all.

The waiter advised me to order a cold lager, which was more similar to what I would have been used to in South Africa. Apart from this small mishap and the fact that my favourite cigarette, Mills, was not obtainable in England, there were no further annoying incidents.

Sarah decided that she wanted to wash her hair and get ready for our evening meal we were going to have in the hotel dining room. For Sarah, this was such an occasion. I think she wanted to look her best.

I told her to simply ring room service if she needed anything, even if she thought her dress required ironing. To escape this titivating, I decided to go to the bar for a lager and listen to the local gossip.

There were only a few people in the bar, but to my amazement, there was an African gentleman dressed in a dark suit who seemed especially familiar. I was sure it was the same man I met at Vuzi's grandfather's home back in South Africa.

I tried not to make eye contact, but the man came over and stood next to me and spoke. 'You must have found our diamonds then, seeing that you are here in England in this lovely hotel. We must have those diamonds as our organisation relies on them for funding.'

In my defence, I explained, 'We never found any of your diamonds, but we found some gold coins from the *Grosvenor* wreck. That's how we managed to come to England.'

He responded, 'Likely story. We will be watching you and will know if you try to sell any of those diamonds.'

I replied, 'You can watch all you like. I have nothing to sell.'

Placing a card on the table, he proclaimed, 'It would be wise to contact us. Think it over but remember we will find you anywhere.'

With that he walked away, leaving me to stare at his card and wondering how they tracked us down. They must have been watching the airport. Vuzi was right all along; these are wicked men. I thought I better not tell Sarah of this incident as it would only frighten her.

Finishing my beer, I returned to our room and met by Sarah, now in an evening dress, her hair done, ready to stun all in the restaurant. 'You look beautiful; I love you and will be proud to escort you downstairs,' I expressed with delight.

We had a lovely meal; I could see Sarah was genuinely enjoying the majestic and luxurious surroundings, which made me extremely happy. The Russell Hotel is located on the surprisingly quiet Russell Square, even though it is in central London. It was next to a beautiful park, near restaurants and pubs, and not too far a walk to Covent Garden or the theatres. I suggested we go to one of the many theatres as it would be a new experience for Sarah, and she was already suitably dressed for the London nightlife.

The following morning while waiting for Mr Cohen's driver to pick us up, I explained to Sarah, 'As soon as we get an apartment and settled, I want to enrol you in a music school or find you a music teacher. You have a great talent, and it is a priority to develop it to the best of your ability.'

Sarah cuddled up to me. 'I love you, and I also appreciate what you are trying to do for me, but if truth be told, I purely want to be with you and care for you.'

A nice-looking young man approached us. 'Hello, are you James and Sarah? My name is Jack. I work for Mr Cohen and have come to collect you.'

Jack drove us to a suburb called Hampstead, where Mr Cohen's store was situated. Sarah was extremely impressed by the quality of the clothing for sale; it was mostly ladies' clothing from top brands such as Aquascutum, Eskada and Jaeger. There was also a small section of men's clothing, all carrying the Jaeger brand. Squeezing my hand, Sarah gaped, 'I wouldn't mind working here amongst all these beautiful clothes.'

We then went to Mr Cohen's office on the top floor. He greeted us with a friendly smile. 'I hope you had a good night's rest and refreshed from your long trip. Two parcels have also arrived for you. Let me show you around the store, and then we can go to the bank to open your accounts.

Afterwards, I will take you to view a small bedsit apartment I found for you, not too far from the store. I think this apartment will be acceptable in the short term until you are well established and know your way around London.'

Opening the bank account was a mere formality, and our chequebook and bankers card would arrive by post in about a week. The apartment was a few blocks away from the store, within easy walking distance, and situated on the second floor of an old Victorian house, divided into flats, with the owner living on the ground floor.

It consisted of a large room that served as a bedroom, lounge, and a built-in counter and four stools partitioned a small section that acted as the kitchen—featuring a separate bathroom and toilet. It was fully furnished and entirely respectable. Sarah loved it. After paying a deposit, Mr Cohen arranged with the landlady for us to move in the following day. The cost of living at the Russell Hotel would soon deplete the cash we had; it was especially advantageous

The next morning we moved into our apartment, and Sarah decided to go shopping to fill the small fridge/freezer with provisions. In her absence, I opened the two parcels received by Mr Cohen on our behalf and carefully removed the diamonds, storing them in four small bags I had for the purpose. The four bags I distributed evenly into the money belt that I bought in a duty-free shop. I decided to keep it permanently on my person until I found a buyer.

Sarah returned full of laughter and smiles. 'You know, James, I am happy. Everything is truly working out perfectly, and I can't wait to start work in Mr Cohen's store, surrounded by all those beautiful outfits. My mother would be green with envy.'

I grinned. 'Tomorrow we must get you a few of those beautiful outfits to wear to work.' Mr Cohen stated we only had to pay the cost price as it was good advertising if the sales staff wears the same clothing as sold in the store. He also confirmed we could start work on Monday.

That afternoon we went into central London to a telephone call office as you could not make overseas calls from a call box. We phoned our parents to let them know that we had arrived safely. This was expensive and inconvenient. I decided there and then to have a private phone installed in our apartment as I was foreseeing regular overseas phone calls.

That evening we spent at home with a bottle of wine, watching the TV that was part of the furnishing of our apartment. There were many new things to take in, making even the most straightforward experience exciting.

The following Monday we headed off to work, with Sarah in a new Eskada outfit looking like a million dollars. Sarah was to help and learn all about clothing in a well-established ladies' outfitter. On the other hand, I had to manage the men's section, which although it was part of the same store, but with a separate entrance.

The men's section had until this point been unstaffed, and the few customers that they did have served by one of the salesladies from the ladies' department. Mr Cohen was hoping that sales would improve if he had a male salesperson dedicated to that section.

I thought that Mr Cohen was simply trying to help as he promised his brother in South Africa. It did not concern me as after the first day; I realised that this was not the occupation for me, standing in a shop all day waiting for a customer to walk in.

Sarah, however, was blissfully happy helping rich ladies select beautiful outfits. It was as if she was born into selling expensive, fashionable clothes produced by leading fashion houses and could not wait each morning to go to work.

CHAPTER SIXTEEN

During the first week at work, I met a guy called Howard, who was reasonably well off and in the import-export business. To me, this sounded like the area that I wanted to get involved in, and soon a friendship developed, and we formed a loose partnership.

Howard was in his mid-thirties with light brown hair, blue eyes, and a pleasant smile. He came from Vienna but had the use of an office in London. With contacts all over and knew immediately where I could sell my uncut diamonds. He had a connection in Zurich, Mr Ahman, who owned a precious metal refinery but also dealt in diamonds.

Mindful of the warning given by the African man I met in the Russell Hotel, I thought that selling the diamonds in Switzerland was a good idea; hopefully, nobody would have anticipated such a move. Howard also advised me that it would be a good idea to open a bank account in Zurich to avoid the massive tax burden if I brought the proceeds of the sale back to England.

Howard had alerted Mr Ahman to the fact that I would call, which smoothed the introduction. When I spoke with him, he seemed to be an amicable person and stated his interest in purchasing the diamonds.

We arranged to meet the following week in Zurich at the Credit Suisse Bank used by Mr Ahman. He also recommended that I open an account at the same bank to expedite the transaction.

After arranging a few days off work, I said to Sarah. 'You know that if I receive a fair amount of money for these diamonds, I won't be going back to work.

Instead, I will concentrate on giving this import-export business a go with Howard. Him being in Vienna and me here in London.

Now that the phone is connected, I could work from home and only use the office for meetings and as our business address. I don't feel my future lies in, as a men's clothing retailer.'

With a loving look in her big, round eyes, Sarah replied, 'As long as you are happy and you know what you're doing. As for me, I would like to stay where I am. I find selling and outfitting my lady customers with beautiful clothing enormously rewarding. My music teacher is also an incredibly kind and talented person; I enjoy my lessons and am hoping to get a gig in a local pub. James, I am so glad we came to England. I am happy; it has opened up a whole new world for me.'

Taking Sarah in my arms, I remarked, 'Your happiness to me is the most important thing in life. You know I love you.'

'I love you too and can't wait for our wedding day,' Sarah replied, cuddled up to my chest.

Although my first love was to become a computer programmer, I felt that it was my duty to build up a firm financial footing to protect both Sarah and myself. The import-export business seems to be the right direction.

The following week I departed for Zurich on Swiss Air, where I took a cab to my hotel in Bahnhof Strasse, conveniently situated on the same street as the Credit Suisse Bank where I was due to meet Mr Ahman.

The bank was imposing and reeked of old money. I was escorted to the first floor by someone who seemed to me like a butler. Everything was wood-panelled and a bit overwhelming. I was showed into a private room occupied by four gentlemen, obviously not bank employees as they were younger and a lot more colourful.

An elderly, stocky man stood up with his hand outstretched to me. 'My name is Siegfriet Ahman, and these are my associates, who are experts in diamonds. They assist me with all purchases. I hope you had a good flight.'

After I greeted everyone present, Mr Ahman asked me to give the stones to his colleagues, to commence examining them while we had a cup of tea and a good chat.

Having removed my money belt in the hotel, I handed them the four bags of diamonds. All the stones were spread out on a black cloth and repeatedly photographed. Mr Ahman professed that was to remove the temptation of theft.

I had also secretly photographed all the stones and counted them in my hotel room but was pleased that Mr Ahman was cautious and tried to act justly.

All this time, the procedure, observed by a bank official, merely standing there. I thought that this bank was exceptionally intimidating and similar to my headmaster office at school. At any minute, they will reprimand you for doing something wrong.

Mr Ahman took me to one side where we relaxed and had some tea. There was no milk offered, and the tea was watery and weak looking. I thought it best not to comment, and I took the occasional sip to appear friendly but found it most disgusting.

Mr Ahman, however, was an especially exciting person, and I knew that I had made a valuable contact. He seemed to deal in all sorts but was particularly interested in diamonds, gold, and oil.

Realising my South African connection, he mentioned he would buy any number of Krugerrands on offer. I told him of my adventure finding the gold coins from the *Grosvenor* wreck and confirmed that there might be more to salvage.

After what seemed like an eternity and several cups of awful tea, Mr Ahman's experts called him over. They had a demonstrative discussion in German, which I could not follow at all even though I took German at school and could speak fluent Afrikaans.

Mr Ahman returned and asked me, 'What sort of figure did you have in mind for these stones?'

Feeling a bit unsure, I replied, 'I thought about a quarter of a million pounds.'

Mr Ahman responded, 'These stone will be worth a lot of money when they are cut and polished, but in their raw state I can only offer you a £130,000.'

'£150,000 sterling and they are yours,' I quickly countered.

With some hesitation, Mr Ahman gave in. 'Okay, I will take them. Have you thought of how you would like payment?'

I was relieved and pleased as I had only anticipated a third of what he offered. 'I would like to open two accounts in this bank, one in dollars and another in British pounds. Ten thousand pounds in cash and the balance divided into these two bank accounts.'

Mr Ahman called the bank official over, who summoned a young lady to take my particulars. Her name was Anje, and she was also personally in charge of my accounts. I could phone her and, after an identity check, instruct her as to what transaction I would like relating to my accounts.

Anje returned with my ten thousand pounds, two business cards with her telephone number, and each bank account number. She also gave me a telex number, and the two deposit slips as proof of the money paid into my accounts.

With that Mr Ahman stood up, saying, 'Thank you, James, it was a pleasure doing business with you. Can I now invite you for a meal?'

'It would be a pleasure,' I replied, following Mr Ahman out of the room and leaving his associates behind to tidy up.

We had a most satisfying meal in the Schweizerhof Hotel, after that drinking several cognac brandies and discussing business until midnight.

CHAPTER SEVENTEEN

The following morning, I set off to the airport to catch my flight back to London with the ten thousand pounds safely tucked into my money belt.

I was delighted with the outcome of the transaction. Also that I had established a contact such as Mr Ahman. These were extremely scarce as the majority of people in this business only acted as go-betweens.

I also thought that this money would enable me to buy a house for Sarah, and we could now get married. Bringing a warm feeling all over, and I smiled, thinking of the joyful look on Sarah's lovely face.

After taking the Underground to my nearest station, I strolled down the road to our apartment with my mind still far away and full of plans. I was brought down to earth by a policeman who prevented me from entering my building.

'Sorry, sir, you can't go in,' the policeman commanded.

'But I live here,' I replied, totally confused.

'What are your name and apartment number?' he enquired. 'I will call a senior officer. It is a crime scene, and nobody is to enter without permission.'

After taking this information from me, he spoke to someone over his walkie-talkie and soon another police officer appeared.

'My name is Detective Sergeant Ashton. I have some bad news. Your partner, Miss Sarah Meth, has died. The truth is, it is murder. She tried to prevent a burglary, and got fatally stabbed in the process.'

His words painfully etched themselves on my brain like a sculptor with a chisel. I was overwhelmed by the urge to fold over; it was only my adrenaline willing me upright that prevented me from fainting.

'Oh my God, when and why did this happen?' I exclaimed, panicking, knowing from that instant, the world as I knew it, had changed again.

'The doctor estimated around 9 pm last night. In your absence, Mr Cohen has identified her for us. It seems that she was returning from her music lessons and found someone busy ransacking the place. We don't know if they took anything. Maybe you could give us a better idea?

Please come with me, and I will show you, but please don't touch anything, the forensic team is still busy collecting evidence. I must also ascertain your whereabouts last night, especially around 9 pm?'

'I have presently returned from a meeting with a friend in Zurich. You can have my used airline tickets if you like,' I explained, handing them over.

Entering the apartment, I had to brace myself. The scene that confronted me was chaos: everything was ripped apart and strewn over the floor. Most upsetting was the tell-tale chalk mark, and blood spatters where they found Sarah's body.

Detective Ashton commented, 'They made a complete mess. From my experience, I would say that they were looking for something in particular. Do you have any idea what they were after, or can you see if anything is missing in this mess?'

Trying to stay calm, I conceded, 'It must be money. We had a large sum in cash, but I still have that on me in my money belt. Other than that, I can't say everything is in such a state. Sarah must have caught them in the act of going through our things.'

'That is what we suspected. Your landlord saw two African men leaving the premises around the time this happened. We are now questioning everyone in the area to assist in compiling an identikit of them. What I don't understand is why did they target you, and if it was the money, how did they know?'

Shaking my head, I replied, 'I have no idea why anyone should target us or kill Sarah; she was the sweetest girl in the world.'

It was as if a great dark cloud was hanging over me. I felt entirely responsible for Sarah's death, thinking that it must be the ANC guy who confronted me in the Russell Hotel looking for the diamonds. I did not want to tell the police of my suspicions as this would reveal the fact that I had smuggled diamonds into the country. This matter would have to be dealt with privately as I was adamant that they should not be allowed to get away with this deed.

Detective Ashton responded. 'I have many years of experience, and my instinct tells me that this is no ordinary burglary attempt.' He noticed that I was unsteady on my feet and turning a greyish colour, he steadied me and called one of the constables. 'Please take Mr Hammond to the local hotel and help him to check-in and lie down for a while.' To me, he instructed, 'Check in to this hotel. I will see you later. Under no circumstances are you to leave the premises without my permission.'

I followed the constable in a trance to the local hotel, booked in and opened the bottle of whisky I had stowed in my suitcase, bought from a duty-free store at the airport.

The undiluted whisky had a numbing effect on me, replacing my distress with anger. Mr Ahman will help, I thought. He seems to have contacts everywhere.

Regardless of whether Mr Ahman could help or not, these guys will receive punishment even if I had to do it myself. Nobody was going to do this to my Sarah and get away with it. Especially not these terrorists. What were they thinking? We were not in Africa.

After several whiskies, my anger subsided, replaced by a great sadness. Tears now ran freely down my cheeks as I wondered what I would do without Sarah. I loved her dearly, and everything I did was for her. Maybe taking the diamonds was going a bit too far, but that was to secure our future.

Now there was no future, only loneliness, I thought as I took another mouthful of the amber liquid. Happily, the alcohol had the right effect on me and soon I was sound asleep, still fully dressed, and lying awkwardly across the bed.

I woke up feeling dizzy, my eyes taking a moment to adjust to the early morning light. After a few moments, the cloud in my brain seems to lift, revealing all the memories of yesterday.

With a start, I jumped out of bed. 'Oh my God, Sarah's mother! I have forgotten to tell her what has happened.' Time zones, I thought, will she be up yet? Realising that South Africa was only one hour ahead, I booked my call. The hotel receptionist revealed it would be about twenty minutes.

Waiting for the call to come through, I was nervously preparing what to say, the anticipation making me panic-stricken, knowing full well that Sarah's mother would be distraught.

The phone rang, giving me a start. Fortuitously, it was Mr Meth. Relieved, I explained to him what happened, begging their forgiveness and stressing how dreadfully sorry I was. Mr Meth took my number, saying that he would call back within an hour. They needed time to digest what had happened.

I got dressed and headed towards the dining room for breakfast, stopping at reception to let them know where I was in case of any phone calls.

I had scarcely started on my orange juice, Mr Cohen appeared. 'James, I am sorry about Sarah. All of the staff at the store send their condolences.'

I replied, 'Please thank everyone for me. It is a devastating loss; I don't know what I am going to do without Sarah.'

'I can't imagine how you feel. Take your time before you make any decision. I also know you can't stay here or go back to your apartment. I have contacted the local council and explained what happened. Because of your grief, the Council is willing to let you jump the queue and can offer you a two-bedroom apartment immediately. You have to go to the Council offices, view the apartment and if you like it, sign all the necessary paperwork,' Mr Cohen explained.

A bit embarrassed, I replied, 'I don't know what to say. It is exceedingly kind of you to go to all this trouble. But I must say this certainly shines a light at the end of a dreadfully dark tunnel. I had no idea which way to turn, and this will give me some direction.'

Mr Cohen gave me a slip of paper with contact details of the local council. 'The council also informed me that there would be a grant to help you purchase furniture. You will find that their apartments are well maintained and inexpensive. Also, don't even think of coming to work until you feel completely ready. I shall now leave you to enjoy your breakfast. If you need any help, please do not hesitate to call me.'

After Mr Cohen left, I sat thinking that there were some good people around. I was dreading going back to our old apartment and, although this hotel was indeed comfortable, it was far too expensive for us working class.

I pushed aside my plate of half-eaten scrambled eggs on toast, deciding to return to my room and await the call from Mr Meth. I was not feeling hungry anyway.

What perfect timing, the phone started ringing as soon as I opened my room door. I picked up the receiver and recognised Mary's voice, the telephonist at the Lusikisiki post office. 'Hello, James, please hold for Mr Meth.'

Her voice was crystal clear as if she was in the same room. She startled me; I had forgotten the dangers back home, realising I will have to be careful in what I mentioned as the exchange staff in Lusikisiki will eavesdrop.

Mr Meth came on the line. 'Do you know when the funeral will be? Sarah's mother is coming over. I will let you know the flights and time of arrival.'

I replied, 'I am sure there will be an inquest first. At this point, I have no further information other than what I told you this morning. I believe that I am getting a two-bedroom apartment. Mrs Meth is welcome to stay with me.' Mr Meth confirmed that it would be a good idea as we didn't know how long she would have to stay.

I then phoned Detective Ashton to let him know that I would be absent for the rest of the day as I was going to see the local council about an apartment. The detective made an appointment for ten o'clock the following morning.

I took a taxi to the local council offices and introduced myself. They were exceptionally sympathetic, and within a half-hour, I was viewing the apartment. It was in a small block of flats, three stories high and not far from the old apartment. It also overlooked a lovely park, and the surroundings seemed pleasant.

The apartment itself was far superior to the old one, having a luxury kitchen, a separate bathroom, two decent sized bedrooms, a lounge and dining room with a lovely balcony overlooking the park. All this for £9.00 per week including rates on an assured tenancy; I was impressed, and I signed immediately.

Even the phone in the apartment was working. I contacted BT and asked them to transfer my number from the old apartment to this new address. BT assured me that they would complete this by the following day.

The council also offered a grant to repaint the apartment and to assist with furnishing. I was delighted I visited a used furniture store where I managed to purchase a three-piece suite, a TV, a dining room table and chairs, a fridge-freezer, cooker, and a washing machine, all within the grant. The two beds I decided to purchase new as I thought second-hand mattresses were a bit dodgy.

Returning to the hotel that evening, I felt a bit better and was pleased with the day's work. After a pleasant meal, I went to the bar and had several whisky's.

The next morning Detective Ashton, accompanied by a constable, arrived to take my statement. It was a mere formality and took no time at all. He also gave me a progress report; it seemed that no further information as to the identity of the two intruders was available and that they were continuing with their enquiries.

Detective Ashton still felt that there was more to this attempted robbery, explaining to me his thoughts and handing over his business card. He asked me to contact him at any time if I felt that I could shed more light as to the reason behind the burglary.

I informed him of my new address and telephone number as I was planning to move to my new apartment that day. He also notified that they would contact me in the next few days to let me know when

Sarah's body would be released, to arrange her funeral.

The rest of the day I spent moving from shop to apartment, buying all sorts of bedding, curtains, and crockery. All this activity kept my mind active and pushed all thoughts of Sarah to one side until I went to the old apartment to collect our belongings.

The police had finished with their forensic examinations and did an excellent job of tidying up and cleaning. The apartment seemed dark and gloomy, and everything I touched reminded me of Sarah. I could not wait to get out, and by the time I was finished the dark cloud smothering me had returned.

Immediately on my arrival at the new apartment, I reached for my bottle of whisky and had several neat measures until I felt in control of myself.

I phoned Mr Cohen and asked him to call back to see if my phone number transferred had gone through to my new apartment. Relieved that the phone rang a few seconds later, I explained to him how delighted I was with the new apartment, thanking him for arranging everything and how impressed I was with the friendly service of the council.

I then booked a call to Mr Meth to inform him of my new contact details. Mr Meth told me that Sarah's mother would be arriving the following Monday morning at Heathrow Airport and asked me to meet her there. I agreed and also assured Mr Meth that they did not have to worry about accommodation as my apartment was big enough to accommodate her.

I nearly forgot about my mother. When I got through to her and explained what happened, she was devastated and offered to come over. I explained to her that Sarah's mother was on her way and that there was no need for her to turn up as well. It would be much nicer if she came over after everything calmed down, for a holiday. That would cheer me up a lot.

One more task, I thought, finding the card handed to me by the ANC man at the Russell Hotel. On the card was the name Zaba Mthetwa and a London telephone number. I first called Howard in Vienna and then Mr Ahman in Zurich, telling them the whole story, and asked them to help in punishing this Mr Mthetwa.

They both agreed to help me in sorting this man out. Mr Ahman stated that he had bought diamonds before from these ANC guys and knows that they are a terrible bunch who could not be trusted.

Satisfied by what I had accomplished that day, I poured another whisky and turned the television on to find a relaxing programme. I found I could not concentrate; it was lonely in the apartment without Sarah, who kept on entering my thoughts with every scene I watched on the TV. Taking the bottle of whisky with me to the bathroom, I decided to have a long, relaxing bath and a few more drinks.

Two hours later I awoke stone-cold sober in an ice-cold bath. I turned on the hot water tap to slowly allow my body to thaw out—what a waste of good whisky.

The funeral director received Sarah's body, and I asked them if they could make her nice-looking as I was sure Mrs Meth would want to say her last farewell. Funeral arrangments scheduled for the next Wednesday at the local crematorium.

I survived the next few days in a whisky-induced trance, feeling sorry for myself and dreading the arrival of Sarah's mother. I felt responsible for taking Sarah from the safety of their house to England, only for her to pass away in this faraway place.

Monday arrived, I took great care to stay off the alcohol that morning as I had to meet Mrs Meth at Heathrow Airport. She was exceptionally quiet but did smile at me. Thus reassured, I led her to the underground to catch a tube home.

Happening to be Mrs Meth's first trip out of the Transkei, she was taken aback by all the people and houses. On our arrival at the apartment, she asked, 'Why are the houses joined together? And your apartment, you got families below and above you. Does it get noisy? It must do at night. It is a lovely apartment, though.'

I replied, 'It does not get noisy, the buildings are all soundproof. You must remember this is an island and space is at a premium.

Mrs Meth, I feel bad having gone to all the trouble to bring Sarah out here, and then this happens. I fully understand if you resent me as I feel responsible for Sarah's death. If I had suspected that this might happen, I never would have brought her here.'

She took my hand. 'Dear James, don't punish yourself, I know that you loved her and I honestly believe that it is God's decision when our time is due. Sarah wanted to come to England, and I am sure she was thrilled being here, even though it was for such a short time. Now, let's have some tea and not another word of remorse.

It sure is lovely to do and go where one likes, without feeling like a criminal. I cannot understand the mentality of the people in South Africa, not wanting all the people regardless of their race, to share the abundant resources of the country. If England, with this large population in such a small area, can do this successfully, certainly South Africa can achieve the same harmony that seems to exist here between races.'

I replied, 'It is not the country, but fascist people who either out of fear or self-importance decide on racial segregation. Let's forget about that stupid country for now. I would like to take you to Sarah's work to meet her boss. He has been exceptionally kind to us, and Sarah was proud of where she worked. After that, we can visit Sarah at the undertakers to say our goodbyes, who informed me that they had made her beautiful and dressed her in her favourite outfit.'

Arriving at the clothing store where Sarah worked, Mrs Meth exclaimed, 'Wow, this is incredibly upmarket! Sarah must have been in her element here. She always liked nice things.'

Mr Cohen was delighted to meet her and showed her around the store. He helped her to select an outfit for the funeral at staff discount. The smile on Mrs Meth's face radiated her pleasure, uplifting the whole occasion.

Arriving at the funeral parlour was a much more sombre experience. Still, I was pleased seeing Sarah for the first time after the knife attack that there were no signs of injury and that she looked beautiful, serene, and peaceful.

Mrs Meth and I held hands as we bid our farewells to Sarah, and I wondered how we would cope with this significant loss. Her whole life, removed like the tide obliterates footprints in one single sweep on a sandy beach. Tears welled up in my eyes as the realisation hit me that this would be the last time that I saw my beautiful brown-eyed girl and that, from now on, I would be on my own.

Although Mrs Meth assured me that it was the will of God that took Sarah away, I was not that religious and looked at life more factually. I felt responsible as I had brought Sarah to England, and it was here she was murdered. To crown it all, I was sure that they killed her because of the diamonds I liberated from the ANC smugglers.

With silence like a cloud hanging over us, I took Mrs Meth to a nearby tea room for cakes and tea. She broke the silence, saying, 'This sure is a lovely country. You know, this is the first time in my life that I have visited a tea room and served by friendly white people. Even so, I have thought that after the cremation I would like to take Sarah's ashes back to our smallholding and scatter them in a stream amongst the woods where Sarah spent much time as a child. I think she belongs there even though I am positive she must have loved it here.'

I replied, 'It probably is the right decision as who knows now where I am going to end up, and Sarah should rest close to the people she loved. I don't think there would be any legal problems in doing this. Perhaps you should phone the airline and ask them what the procedure is.'

The following day we spent in preparation for the cremation and finding premises to serve tea and cake to all the people attending. All the staff from Sarah's work were coming, her music teacher, and the owners of the pub where Sarah was going to perform, even a Catholic priest.

Mrs Meth and I were amazed at the number of people Sarah had touched in her short stay in England. We had to hire a conference room at a local hotel that also took care of the catering and charged us per head for the people attending, taking an enormous load off our shoulders, giving us time to prepare speeches and select Sarah's favourite music.

The next day's weather heralded Sarah's funeral. It was thoroughly miserable, with slight drizzle and grey skies that did nothing to ease the occasion. I was in a daze from the moment I woke up and feeling sorry for myself. The hearse with Sarah's body was to meet us in front of the apartment at 11 am; we were then to follow it in Mr Cohen's car to the crematorium.

The chapel at the crematorium offered a beautiful and calm environment to bid Sarah farewell. Mr Cohen acted as the officiant and conducted the introduction, and Sarah's mother and I chose all the music. Mrs Meth also read out a tribute to Sarah. The committal and closing words were made by Mr Cohen, while Mrs Meth and I each placed a rose on Sarah's coffin.

During all this, I felt like I was on another astral plane and that it was not real. Even when Mrs Meth read out her tribute and poem, I was unmoved. Only when the coffin started moving through the curtains did the whole situation hit me, and I was overwhelmed by great sorrow and tears began welling up in my eyes.

I found it challenging to keep my composure after the cremation, frustrated by the chit-chat and condolences from all the people enjoying their tea and cake. I could not wait to go home and get away from all the mourners, pretending how sorry they were for my loss when, in reality, they hardly knew me. I desperately craved stillness and a lie down as I was feeling unsteady on my feet. Mrs Meth, who was coping better at entertaining the guests, noticed my distress and arranged a lift home for me, stating that she would follow later.

Once home, I pulled off my tie and jacket, flinging them onto a chair. Enjoying the familiar silence of the apartment, I welcomed the peace that blocked the noise and tension of the outside world. I poured a double whisky and cried my heart out. Relieved that I was now in my new apartment and thinking it would have been impossible to cope if I had to return to the old apartment where Sarah died.

Hundreds of thoughts were running through my head, from the first moment I met Sarah until the very end. Wondering what would be the way forward now without Sarah's lovely smile, and thinking, what is the point of carrying on, except my desire for revenge? I promised myself again that Sarah's death would not go unpunished.

I decided to suspend all thoughts of revenge until Mrs Meth had returned to South Africa. After a few whisky's, I was feeling a lot like my old self, ready to face the world again.

Mrs Meth's flight was due Friday evening. I got on well with Mrs Meth, but I felt that her presence was a constant reminder of Sarah. She also unwittingly prevented me from consuming my desired amount of whisky.

Even though we were a bit subdued, I insisted that we visit the most popular attractions while she was here in London, it might be her only chance as the flights to England were extremely expensive.

Making sure her camera was fully loaded, we set off to see Buckingham Palace, the Tower of London and Westminster Abbey. She was especially impressed, and we took loads of photos.

What excited her most was wandering down Oxford Street and browsing through the many stores. She was also impressed by the Underground, watching the millions of people of all nationalities coexisting, all in a hurry going somewhere, Lord only knows where. She would have been happy, riding the Underground all day.

I am sure, however, that she was relieved as the time of her flight approached that Friday evening; all the walking must have tired her to no end. We said our goodbyes and promised to stay in touch.

CHAPTER EIGHTEEN

I made my way back home to be welcomed by an empty apartment, missing Sarah's presence every which way I turned. Even a simple thing like turning on the television reminded me of her thrilled look the first time she saw it. Oh, dear God, the emptiness in my life, the devastating loneliness. The silence where there used to be laughter, the permanent blank in my bed.

I felt that my immediate death would be no great disaster. Half of myself had gone; the fulfilled, joyful investment of my love for Sarah had disappeared into the darkness. When Sarah was with me, I seem to overcome all my fears and felt brave enough to stand up to anybody or any situation.

Now, the only promise that seemed to help me snap out of this depressed mood was whisky. After the second glass, the clouds in my mind would part, filling the overwhelming emptiness slowly with sweet thoughts and the pleasure of revenge.

I slowly started to realise that whisky was becoming too important in my life and that if I didn't snap out of my depressed state soon, there would be no turning back. Mindful of this, I decided to put all my efforts into trying to build an import-export business and to plan revenge for Sahra's murder without having to use whisky as a psychological crutch.

I contacted Mr Cohen, thanking him again for all the help he had given me and explained to him that I would not be returning to work in his store as I was not suited for the retail business. Instead, I was going to concentrate on international trade as I had several opportunities offered to me.

One such opportunity was that my associate, Howard, was importing orchids from Thailand and selling them to the local flower markets in Vienna where he lived. He thought that London also presented a good market as they were selling in the *Covent Garden* flower market for £1.99, and my landed cost would be five US cents per orchid. He had previously toyed with the thought of doing this himself. But it would be too difficult to control from far away because Covent Garden operated on a sale or return basis; if you were not on the spot to check on purchases, you would never be sure whether you were being duped or not.

Mr Cohen thought that was a good idea and offered to introduce me to a few Covent Garden flower sellers he knew. He also asked that I inform him of any other opportunities I received as he would be interested. I told him that I had a buyer for Krugerrands who would be willing to pay the going rate without charging a commission.

Mr Cohen's face lit up. He expressed that he had many friends who would be interested in selling and that I must investigate this further. He would be keen to meet the buyer if possible and stated that I should negotiate a commission; he would make sure that I remain protected on every transaction he arranged.

I felt especially excited and reassured that I made the right decision in pursuing the import-export business. Through Mr Cohen's introduction, I visited three traders in Covent Garden who were keen to sell my orchids. I ordered the first consignment, one box, purely to try out the market. Because of all the paperwork involved at Heathrow Airport to clear the orchids, I decided to appoint a clearing agent, giving me more time to distribute and find additional outlets.

Between the three traders, I sold the first box on the same day, encouraging me to increase my order to three boxes, one box each. I did not think that this was a big gamble as the orchids had a shelf life of fourteen days, and each orchid came with its own small plastic water container.

I soon built a network of outlets and was importing ten boxes of orchids per day, which kept me busy with visiting traders, delivering their orders, and monitoring sales each day. I did not think of revenge for the next three weeks until I received a call from Howard stating that he and Mr Ahman were coming over as they thought they had tracked down the African man who threatened me about the diamonds.

Mr Ahman was keen on horse racing and suggested that we meet that Saturday at Newmarket Racecourse.

As I had never been to a horse race, I phoned Mr Cohen to ask what sort of outfit was customary at these events. He replied, 'Come to the store, and I will find you something suitable. I am also going to Newmarket on Saturday as I own a racehorse; he is running in the third race. I am also a member and would be glad to take you and show you around.'

'That would be great. The person I am to meet is Mr Ahman from Zurich who is interested in buying Krugerrands as we discussed. It would be advantageous for the two of you to meet.'

At Mr Cohen's store, he recommended a light grey suit as we would be in the members' area of the racecourse. He stated, 'It might be a bit more formal there, but not so crowded, and you can see better from the stands.'

I was secretly pleased as I needed a more casual suit. My only suit was the black one I wore to Sarah's cremation, and I did not feel like wearing that ever again. The suit he selected was a Jaeger brand of superb cut and made out of pure wool. It felt and looked perfect, justifying the price tag.

That Saturday Mr Cohen's driver took us to Newmarket Racecourse where we met Mr Ahman and Howard as I had prearranged at the members' entrance. Mr Cohen introduced us as his guest and led us to the members' bar.

Champagne was flowing freely while the horse form for each race was discussed by all, displaying their intimate knowledge of each horse. I did not know or understand how to examine the horses' past performance from the racebook and quietly decided that I would simply ask Mr Cohen if his horse stood a chance. If he recommended it, I would make a ten-pound place bet on it.

His horse's name was Skydancer and was due to run in the third race; he thought it stood a fair chance. I decided that would be my selection of the day and duly made a ten-pound place bet.

Howard, peering through his binoculars, called me over. 'Look through my binoculars and tell me if you recognise anyone.' He directed me to look at the bookmaker downstairs on the grass next to the rails where three African men were chatting. 'Why, the guy in the middle is the same African man, Mr Zaba Mthetwa, who threatened me at the Russell Hotel!' I exclaimed.

Howard took the binoculars back. 'That's why we asked you to come to the races, to give us an identity. We discovered our man is keen on gambling and is always at the horse races.'

'Well, that's him. Do you have more information about him?' I responded.

Howard handed me a large, sealed brown envelope and replied, 'This is a full file on your friend. Study it when you get home. Mr Ahman knows all about this guy and is pleased to help. Phone me when you have absorbed all the information, and then we can discuss how to proceed. It seems that now is not the time as Mr Ahman and Mr Cohen are in deep discussion, I think about Krugerrands. Anyway, they seem to be getting along incredibly well.'

Skydancer won his race, creating a lot of excitement, and everyone congratulated Mr Cohen. Mr Ahman even accompanied him to the winner's enclosure where he received his trophy. Mr Ahman placed a lot of money on Skydancer for a win and was in ecstasy. I was sure he was hooked on horse racing, and I would not be surprised if he became a racehorse owner soon. It did seem a great sport and also exceptionally prestigious, well suited for the rich to show off their wealth.

My ten-pound place bet delivered a disappointing return, not even worth the walk to the bookmaker especially as I tried to keep a low profile, not to be spotted by Zaba Mthetwa or his cronies.

After the last race, we all proceeded to the Savoy Hotel in London where Mr Ahman was staying for a celebratory meal and champagne. We decided on Kaspar's Seafood Restaurant, designed in a dazzling Art Deco-style featuring cut-glass mirroring and bright railings, silver-leaf ceiling and a chequerboard marble floor. It was such a far cry from the unsophisticated surroundings of the Royal Hotel Lusikisiki that I was a bit taken aback.

The menu offered a choice from arrays of fresh and smoked fish, Malaysian seafood curry, oysters, caviar, and fresh seafood: delicious slivers of smoked salmon, cured sea bass, or fresh rock oysters followed by Dover sole, lobster, or sea bream; spatchcock, lamb cutlets, or beef. It concluded with clever twists on classic desserts such as apple crème brûlée or Peach Melba sensation.

Although I was not paying, it looked to me as if a meal in this magnificent setting would cost a king's ransom and I settled for the Malaysian seafood curry, thinking that at least it sounded reasonable. It was, without a doubt, the best seafood curry I had tasted in my life, and I was pleased with my choice.

After a most enjoyable meal we set off back to Hampstead in Mr Cohen's car, and Howard accompanied us as he was staying with me. He remarked, 'Mr. Ahman seemed to have thoroughly enjoyed the day racing. He was impressed with Skydancer, and his winnings also helped to make the day.'

Mr Cohen replied, 'Skydancer is a remarkable horse. I have four horses, and without a doubt, he finances the training for all four out of his prize money. Without him, I probably would have got nowhere, but he allowed me to persevere, and consequently, my other two-year-old, Diablo, is now coming into form. He came second last week, and we hope for even better results in the future.'

'It must cost a fortune to train a horse like Skydancer. That is after you raised the finances to buy the horse in the first place. I bet that only the best-bred horse and the best training would give you a possible chance of success. It does not seem to me that investing in a racehorse makes sound business sense. One needs an ulterior motive, like the love of horse racing,' I commented.

Mr Cohen replied, 'The cost involved becomes irrelevant once your horse has won a race. The prize money covers the cost, and the prestige is so uplifting that you feel tempted to buy another horse. Only when you have four or five good horses can you think of it in terms of business. There are a few people who make a lot of money out of owning racehorses. Also, when a winning racehorse retires, there is a stud fee to take into account. However, I must admit that the love of horse racing is the prime motivating factor.'

Mr Cohen's driver pulled up in front of my apartment. I thanked him once again for a lovely day and stated that I would love to do it again soon, if possible. As I guided Howard to my apartment, he commented, 'Your Mr Cohen is an exceedingly interesting man. You are fortunate to have such contact.'

'I know,' I replied. 'Mr Cohen has helped me a lot since I arrived here in England. His brother is my parents' neighbour in South Africa. He arranged even this apartment.'

Howard, relaxing on the sofa, replied, 'It is a nice apartment; I can see that it is well maintained, in a peaceful area, and overlooking a lovely park. I wouldn't mind having one myself. How does one go about applying to rent such an apartment?'

'I think you have to apply to Camden Town Council. They then put you on a waiting list. I got this one immediately because of the crisis with Sarah, which left me in effect, homeless.'

Howard replied, 'Oh well, I will simply have to stay with you when I visit London, and in turn, you can stay with me when you are in Vienna or even in Zurich. I have an apartment there too.'

I poured us each a whisky and relaxed in my armchair, fiddling with the TV remote to find an exciting programme. Howard commented, 'Mr. Ahman wants to discuss what we are going to do about Mr Mthetwa, as he thinks that he is a psycho and extremely dangerous. He also thinks that Mr Mthetwa believes that the diamonds you sold are his, and don't even belong to the ANC. Although he has no proof that you sold the diamonds, he believes that you came to England financed by the sale of these diamonds.'

I replied, 'That doesn't make any sense. I had already paid for my tickets before I even heard about these diamonds. South Africa is one of the only countries in the world where it is illegal to have uncut diamonds without the correct authorisation. You can't even start digging for diamonds. You need a license to start mining. The Department of Mineral Resources will prosecute you for conducting mining activities without a mining right, and that is a criminal offence. The DeBeers cartel has this industry sewn up; you might as well state that every uncut diamond belongs to them. The penalty for being caught in possession of an uncut diamond is ten years.

Therefore, the ANC stole the diamonds first, and my option was who to give the jewels to if I found them: the ANC, the security police, DeBeers or even the German divers if they were still around. None of these options made any sense to me as nobody could prove ownership and I decided that the finder's keepers law will apply, especially as I already had my plane tickets to England. The discovery of some gold coins that were part of the *Grosvenor* treasure financed my move to England.'

Howard responded, 'I am sure Mr Ahman is aware of the situation and is not concerned as long as the fact that he bought these stones remain confidential since Mr Mthetwa's reactions are exceptionally erratic. What's more, he suggested that you inform the police that you suspect Mr Mthetwa's involvement in Sarah's death as he won't believe that you have no diamonds for sale.

Mr Ahman told me that this Mr Mthetwa is looking for you and is concerned as to what his plans are. This guy is dangerous, and we should do something before he has a chance to react. Reporting him to the police could be the answer as Mr Ahman thinks he is here illegally and this could force him to return to South Africa.'

Frowning, I replied, 'I think the security police also want him in South Africa. Mr Ahman is right, at least if I report him to the police, it will make me seem the innocent party in this lousy mess, and I could get some protection.'

Howard, passing me his empty glass, commented, 'I don't even think he is part of the ANC here in England. Mr Ahman has a lot of dealings with them, and they are keen to disassociate themselves from him, stating that he is a loose cannon and far too violent for their organisation here in England. Whether this was purely talking to keep Mr Ahman happy, I don't know.'

I will have to give this some serious consideration, I thought. If I am the cause of Mr Mthetwa going into hiding because I put the police on to him, he might come after me. 'When do we see Mr Ahman again? I think I will wait until after we see him.'

Howard replied, 'Monday at eleven. He wants to inspect the office facilities I use, with a mind to do the same and then we will go out for lunch. Anyway, let's retire for the night. Tomorrow I have a serious business opportunity we need to discuss.'

With that, we went to our separate rooms. I tossed and turned for some time, worrying if going to the police about Mr Mthetwa was the right thing to do. He had murdered once to my knowledge, was I not only aggravating the situation more? Eventually, I fell asleep, but without getting any nearer to a solution.

CHAPTER NINETEEN

The next morning, I woke up early, tidied the kitchen, and made Howard and myself a cup of tea. I suggested we have breakfast in a café not far from the apartment, leaving the rest of the morning free to discuss Howard's plan.

He wanted me to source ten metric tonnes of butter from Ireland for his client in Iran. He informed me that his client was ready to open a transferable letter of credit immediately. Why he did not only send me a fax request, I did not know. I could only assume that he wanted to monitor the whole exercise in person and that he had some other intention.

Howard was one of the kindest people I knew, with a heart of gold and a brain as sharp as a razor, but below the surface, he also had a criminal streak. He made every transaction into some kind of fraud against the establishment. For instance, I am sure that in this butter deal he had some scheme to claim subsidies from the EU intervention board and that is why he needed me to source the butter, a sort of front. I decided some time ago not to get involved with any of Howard's transactions other than on a commission basis as an agent. That is why we never formed a formal partnership but traded together independently on a loose but friendly basis.

I explained to Howard that I had a contact who could supply the butter and we could complete the transaction by Friday that week. 'I should have prices for you tomorrow, and if accepted, they could issue a pro forma invoice immediately after that.'

Howard grinned. 'That would be perfect. I will give you the name and details to who you should address the invoice.'

The rest of the day passed without any mishaps except for this nagging concern about whether I should report Mr Mthetwa to the police or not. I must admit that I was a bit scared of the consequences; he was a murderer after all.

The following day I discussed the whole matter with Mr Ahman who persuaded me to tell all, except the fact that I found the diamonds, to the police as he felt that it would put me in the clear no matter what Mr Mthetwa did. Besides, he thought it was better for my safety as Mr Mthetwa would find me eventually. With the police involved, he might be less keen to attack me.

I found the thought of dealing with the police unpleasant; after all, I had always rebelled against authority, especially the police in South Africa who seemed to me to be no more than bullies. Detective Ashton, however, was a lot more sympathetic and spoke to me as a victim and not treating me as a criminal.

That afternoon I phoned Detective Ashton, who agreed to meet me at my apartment in half an hour. I left Howard and Mr Ahman to continue with the contract for his office and caught a taxi back home. Detective Ashton was already at my door on my arrival. He was wearing a dark suit and a blue striped tie. 'Hi, that was quick; I didn't think you would beat me getting here. You dressed very formally for the occasion.'

Shaking my hand, he replied, 'Hello, James, I was in court all day and did not have time to change. I always think that in cases like this, it is best to deal with them immediately in case the informant changes his mind.'

'Does this happen often?' I enquired.

'You will be surprised. If it is left for twenty-four hours or more, sixty per cent would have decided for one reason or another that it is no longer worth the risk.'

How refreshing, I thought, this guy seems like a human being. I felt at ease in his presence; he was not fresh from the KGB central office. I opened the door widely.

'Well, it's no good discussing the case on the doorstep. Please come inside.' I led the way through to the lounge and pointed to a comfortable chair. 'Please sit down. Can I offer you a drink or a cup of tea? I am going to have a small whisky.'

Grinning, he replied, 'Well, seeing that this is my last call today, I will join you. Please call me Mike. I hate all these formalities. You are not a suspect.'

After we were both seated comfortably, I explained to Mike what had happened. Stressing that I did not suspect this Zaba Mthetwa as it was nonsense to think that I had found these diamonds as he was well aware that he only told me of their existence a week before we left for England. By this time the flights and all the arrangements were already in place, financed by the sale of the gold coins we found diving for the *Grosvenor* wreck.

I did not want to publicise that I sold the gold coins as I was not sure how legal it was taking that amount of money out of South Africa. In my mind, I did not have a choice, as we were not allowed to live together there. In effect, the law made us leave the country; that is the reason why I have not told him the full story before.

Mike, after taking another sip of his whisky, commented, 'James, I don't understand, why were you not allowed to live together?'

'It is a criminal offence for people of different races to live together in South Africa. The government classified Sarah as non-white.'

Nearly choking on his whisky, Mike burst out with, 'My God, that's ridiculous! She was definitely as white as you and me. Not to go into South African law, you selling gold coins and bringing money from there has nothing to do with this case. But tell me why you have come to mention all this now?'

'Well, Mike, I was at the racecourse with a friend when I spotted Mr Mthetwa and pointed him out, telling my friend the story about Sarah and this guy's insinuation about me taking his diamonds. This friend, Mr Ahman from Switzerland, told me to go to the police immediately as he knows about this man and that he is an exceedingly dangerous crook using the ANC set up here in England as a front. He warned me that my life could be in danger as Mr Mthetwa strikes out violently when he does not get his way.'

Mike's eyes lit up. 'That could have been his motive for searching your apartment. I have never had any dealings with this so-called ANC, but I'll check them out. Do you have an address and telephone for Mr Mthetwa? I take it that you would not like me to mention your involvement in this.'

Mike advised me to be careful in case this guy is dangerous. 'I don't know if we could affect an arrest as I am sure that he would have instructed someone else to do his dirty deeds, making it exceedingly difficult to prove his involvement. However, I certainly will investigate him. If we can't get him for murder, perhaps we could arrest him on some other charge.'

I handed Mike another whisky and Mr Mthetwa's address. I thought Mike was a nice enough chap, but I had my doubts as to whether the police would be successful in arresting him. It seemed to me that it was entirely up to me to prove his guilt. But where should I start? I had never done this sort of thing before.

'James, thank you for the drink. I will keep you up to date as to what I discover about Zaba Mthetwa. I know what is on your mind but leave the investigating to me.'

With that, Mike got up, and I escorted him to the door. 'Thank you for listening to me. If I uncover any more leads, I will let you know immediately, but please update me with whatever information you acquire about Mr Mthetwa. Maybe next time we could meet in a pub for a beer if you prefer.'

I returned by taxi to our London office, hoping Howard and Mr Ahman were still there as it was nearly five o'clock. I was greeted by Jane, the receptionist, looking attractive and smart in a long charcoal-coloured jersey over a brown skirt. 'Hello, if you are looking for your associates, they have recently left and instructed I should tell you to meet them at the Savoy Hotel.'

Not knowing what came over me and feeling a bit guilty soon after Sarah's passing, I asked, 'Well, if you are not doing anything, why don't you join us? I could do with some company.'

Not refusing but a bit hesitant, Jane responded, 'I can't possibly go to the Savoy in my work clothes.'

I could see that secretly she wanted to come but simply needed a little persuasion. 'You sure look fine to me. I truly love your outfit. Come, it will be fun.'

'Okay. Give me five minutes to fix my makeup.' Grabbing her bag, she dashed off to the ladies' while I phoned for a taxi.

Although Jane was an enormously attractive blonde with sexy legs, I found that mentally I was still comparing her to Sarah. I had to force myself to try and repress all thoughts of Sarah and acknowledge that Jane was a girl in her own right and had clearly as many good points.

What was I thinking? I hardly knew the girl, and this was not even a date. We were only going to have drinks in the company of Howard and Mr Ahman. Besides, it was far too soon after Sarah for me to be interested in another woman.

Sarah did restore my self-confidence. While she was alive; I hardly had anything to drink. Maybe Jane will do the same to me.

Jane emerged from the ladies' looking fresh and radiant. 'Right. I am ready for the Savoy now. What do you think?'

'I think you look lovely and wonder if the Savoy is ready for you! I will be the envy of all the men there with you by my side.'

I couldn't help notice the sparkle in her eyes as I helped her into the taxi. 'Savoy Hotel, please,' I instructed the driver.

Jane turned her joyful face towards me. 'Do you guys always go to the Savoy for drinks? It's especially upmarket and expensive. I have lived near London all my life, and this will be the first time I've crossed the threshold of the Savoy.'

Thinking that I was glad that Mr Ahman is paying, I responded, 'No, we're only going because Mr Ahman is staying there. My local pub is usually more in my price bracket. Places like the Savoy are only for special occasions. I thought by your appearance that the Savoy would be your regular. Tell me, where is your home town? I know little about you.'

Jane replied, 'Oh, nothing is exciting to tell. I have two brothers. My home is in Folkestone, Kent. I achieved three A-levels at school, went on to finish a diploma in business studies at Canterbury, and now here I am working in London. What about you? I can tell from your accent you are not local.'

'Now that is the most abridged version of a life story I have ever heard. I bet a lot more exciting things have happened to a beautiful girl like you. You are right, though, this is all new to me. I am from South Africa.'

Exactly then we arrived at the Savoy. I paid the driver and protested to Jane, 'This has to stop. I am spending all my money on taxis. Tomorrow I am going to buy a car.'

Jane, smiling at me, asked, 'What kind of car do you have in mind?'

I don't know where it came from, but I found myself replying, 'A Mercedes Benz, I think a sort of sporty one, with two doors only.'

Jane, holding my hand and with sheer joy in her eyes, exclaimed, 'Can I come with? I would like to help you choose; it will be such fun.'

'You are most welcome, but it will only be a second-hand one. I think a new one would be dreadfully expensive. Are you not working tomorrow? It will be a long day visiting all the Mercedes dealers.'

Smiling, Jane replied. 'We can visit as many dealers as you like. Perhaps you could take me out for lunch. I will take the day off and pick you up early in my little Golf. I suggest we each buy a different newspaper and make a list of dealers we could visit. I can't wait; it is not every day I get a chance to shop for a motor car. My old Golf was purely a hand me down from my mother. Oh, I do like shopping.'

We swapped addresses and telephone numbers, with Jane suggesting to pick me up at eight in the morning. Smiling like two co-conspirators, we entered the Savoy and joined Howard and Mr Ahman at their table. Mr Ahman greeted us with a big smile and a twinkle in his eyes. 'Hello, James, I am glad you brought Miss Fisher. If I were younger, I would have beaten you to it.'

Jane enjoyed the compliments. 'Please, call me Jane. What is this too old? You are never too old. Why to me you look only in the prime of your life.'

Mr Ahman bowed as he took her hand and guided her to a chair. 'Thank you for the compliment, but no matter how young I feel inside, I know I could be your grandfather.'

Jane jabbed me in the ribs and whispered. 'I need to check my makeup before I can relax. It was a bit windy outside.'

I escorted Jane to the ladies and re-joined Mr Ahman and Howard.

While Jane was busily titivating herself in the ladies', I explained to Mr Ahman and Howard that I had informed the police of everything regarding Mr Mthetwa, not including, naturally, that I had, found the diamonds. Mr Ahman seemed relieved and commented, 'Now if anything happens, the police will at least know who the bad guys are.'

I ordered a beer and a glass of white wine for Jane, but Mr Ahman stopped me paying, insisted that he would pay as a thank you for the introduction to Mr Cohen. 'I can see Mr Cohen and I are going to do a lot of business. Think of this evening as an advance payment of your commission.'

We had the most enjoyable meal. I could see that Jane had a marvellous time; she was thrilled savouring the atmosphere and the beauty of the Savoy.

Although I felt confident that I had impressed Jane and that the night promised exciting developments, I merely called a taxi for the two of us as the evening came to an end and dropped Jane off at her lodgings.

I think I was still a bit guilty because of Sarah; it was perhaps a bit pathetic on my part as Howard had made plans to stay at the Savoy for the night as he had business to discuss with Mr Ahman.

CHAPTER TWENTY

The next morning at 8 am, Jane knocked at my door armed with several newspapers and dressed in jeans and a white jumper. 'Good morning, beautiful, you look especially sporty. Come inside for some coffee, and we can study the papers to give us an idea of where to go.'

With the papers spread out on the dining room table and sipping our coffee, Jane remarked, 'You know, there are several Mercedes dealers in the north of London, and it shouldn't take us to long to find you your dream car. Look, here is a red sports model nearly in walking distance from your apartment.'

'That's nice. I want a sports model, but it must have a hardtop. Your lovely hair will get spoiled in no time with this weather.'

We compiled a list of the ten closest dealers offering used Mercedes-Benz cars for sale. The first dealer was a relatively small setup with only four cars for sale. One of their vehicles was a two-door hard-top silver Mercedes 230SL Pagoda with a biscuit colour interior. This car was in beautiful condition with a full-service record. I fell in love with this car immediately and also thought that it was a good omen that it was called Pagoda, named for the distinctive roofline and rounded corners of this particular model. The name reminded me of the gold pagoda coins that paid for me to come to England in the first place. The owner of the dealership also offered me a significant discount if I paid in cash.

Grabbing my hand, Jane pulled me away. 'You can't simply buy the first car you see. That's not shopping. We will visit all ten, have lunch, and only then will we make a decision.'

Reluctantly I was steered away, and we visited all the dealers on the list, but my heart kept returning to the first car. Over lunch, I exclaimed, 'I still think that the first car we looked at is the one for me. The condition is great, the shape is called Pagoda, and he is willing to give a large discount for cash.'

Jane replied, 'I must admit I like the silver and biscuit interior. She certainly is a beauty, but where are you going to get such a large amount of cash on short notice?'

'I came prepared. I have it on me,' I responded, tapping my concealed money belt.

'If you give me a moment, I will remove the exact amount in the gents' toilet and then we can return to dealer number one and buy the car. Don't let on that I had the money in my money belt; we will say I went to the bank to withdraw it.'

Coming back from the gents', I put the money on the table. 'Could you keep it in your handbag for me? I think it would be safer.'

Toying with the notes, Jane exclaimed, 'Goodness! I have never seen that much money together in my life. That's more than I earn in a year. Where do you get it all from?'

'That's a long story. Please put it away safely in your handbag, and if you have finished with your meal, we can get this car buying over and done with.'

I was secretly relieved as carrying all the money around was exceedingly worrying. I was glad that I had decided to spend it on a car; at least now I could enjoy it. An hour later, with all the paperwork done, the car was mine.

I followed Jane to her lodgings, where we parked her car to enable the two of us to go for a drive to get the feel of the Mercedes. It was a lovely car: sporty enough to call it a sports car but not over the top like a supercar, and luxurious enough inside to be described as elegant. It came with superb air conditioning and a top-of-the-range sound system.

Jane was in her element. 'I feel like a film star in this car. My poor old Golf will wither away as I will ask you to drive me wherever I need to go to from now on.'

'You know, that's an excellent idea because for your safety I should pick you up, instead of you coming to my apartment. I think I am in a somewhat dangerous situation at the moment.'

Frowning, Jane replied, 'Why, what is going on? Do you need some space; am I coming on too strong?'

'No, nothing of the sort. I like your company and would like you to visit me at my apartment at any time. Right at the present moment, it is not the safest option.'

I could see Jane was a bit miffed by this. Therefore I explained to her everything, including what happened to Sarah.

I concluded with, 'As you can see, until the police arrest this man, I think it is wise to be a little careful. I suppose I could move again as I am sure that he knows where I am staying, but it was because of Sarah's murder that I got this apartment from the council and I wouldn't want to lose it.'

Jane replied, 'You loved her a lot.'

'Yes, I did, that's why I don't want anything like that happening again. Therefore please, let's be careful. I am sure it won't be for too long. You are too precious to me. Let's go somewhere special tonight where I can show you off in our new car.'

Again, I had to check myself. What was I saying? I had only known Jane for a few days. I had seen her on several occasions when I had meetings in our hired office. I always thought that she was beautiful, with her lovely blonde hair and blue eyes, but thus far, we have not even kissed each other on the lips and here I was talking as if we were already an item. Why Sarah only passed away what seemed like a few days ago.

Jane stated, 'I am with you all the way. But I think this fancy car you bought will antagonise this man and we will have to be even more careful.'

I didn't say anything to Jane, but she had hit the nail on the head; the underlying reason that I bought such a beautiful car was to try to provoke Mr Mthetwa. Hopefully, he would react and do something wrong. I knew the only thing I could do to try to expose Mr Mthetwa was to entice him by exploiting his greed. Now I simply needed to bring my car to his attention.

Mr Mthetwa lived in Romford, which was east of Hampstead. He seemed to share the house with several other Africans. Whether this house was his or belonged to the ANC, I did not know. I would simply have to find an excuse to drive past his home frequently, hoping that he noticed me.

We decided to go for a meal at a restaurant near Jane's lodgings as we both needed an early night to be fit for work the following morning. I had a lovely peppered steak, and thoroughly enjoyed Jane's company, saw her to her front door, and headed home. We had progressed to a proper goodnight kiss and a cuddle.

On my arrival home, Howard was already there and insisted on us going downstairs again, allowing him to inspect the car. The car met with his approval as he was smiling from ear to ear. 'She sure is a beauty.

I bet that Mr Mthetwa will be wondering where the money came from.'

'That is my plan to provoke him as much as possible. I hope he does something foolish.'

Howard replied, 'This car will certainly do the trick, but whether it is a wise move, I don't know. Mr Mthetwa and his cronies don't seem to have high regard for the value of life. They appear to be a dangerous lot.'

With that, we returned upstairs to relax with a whisky each as Howard updated me with the latest telexes he picked up from our town office. One was for me from an Irish butter supplier, confirming that he could supply ten metric tonnes at an acceptable price.

I showed Howard, who was delighted and asked me to get a pro forma invoice the following day. I thought to myself that this is the most straightforward transaction I have done thus far, with an expected percentage for me of £17,000, more than I paid for my car.

Howard advised that he would have to leave for Zurich as soon as he receives the proforma invoice as the letter of credit was with the Union Bank of Switzerland and he needed to be there personally to finalise the transaction. He assured me that he would pay my commission into my Swiss bank account.

I was pleased as the flower sales were becoming erratic, and I had to monitor the wholesalers every day to control their orders. Some would sell a whole box in one day, and others struggled to sell a carton in a week. For these stragglers, I could not supply fresh flowers daily as I did not want to supply less than a carton per delivery. It was not worth the effort to divide a box amongst several wholesalers. The labour involved cut down the profit, having to divide each box into several smaller boxes and then delivering them separately to the different sellers. I then had to check their stock daily. I had to cut out the slower selling wholesalers and concentrate only on those who could move a full box within a day or two.

I found it incomprehensible to understand as a new wholesaler would effortlessly move a box of orchids per day for the first few weeks, and then some would slow down to only a few orchids per day. What was most frustrating, some of the wholesalers that I had dropped for not being able to sell a full box had now started requesting stock as their customers were again looking for orchids.

Although the profits were good, the flower business to me was a bit too finicky, and I realised that I would have to diversify into something a bit more stable as a backbone to the commodity trading deals, which were, unfortunately, few and far between.

I decided to investigate the buy-to-let market and, as Jane came from Kent, I thought that it would be a suitable area. The prices were also more reasonable than London, and I thought the lower end of the market—apartments and terrace houses—would be an excellent place to start.

That evening I took Jane out for a meal and explained my idea to her. She was all for it and exclaimed, 'Both my brothers are in the building trade! George, the youngest, is a plasterer and Graham is an electrician. They have both helped my mum and dad renovate a few properties they purchased to help finance their retirement. I am sure they will give you all the advice you need as I know for a fact that my brothers are always looking for work. When I go to visit, all I hear is them moaning that they don't have enough to do.'

'Well, should we go and visit them this weekend and see if they are interested? It would also be nice to meet your family. Then we will have to compile a list of all the auctions in the area as I would like to buy most of the properties at auction.'

Jane was indeed a decent sort of girl, always ready to help and get involved with whatever idea I came up. Our relationship thus far was purely a few cuddles and kissing hello and goodbye. I don't know what was holding me back, as she was a beautiful and bright girl with a lovely figure. In particular, I liked her decisiveness and fast decision making. We worked together well as a team. Her input and observations in whatever we were doing were always constructive and well worth consideration. Maybe Sarah was still too fresh in my mind.

We set off to Folkestone early Saturday morning, enjoying the feel of the Merc, and the absolute power in overtaking pushed you back into the luxurious leather seats. Cruising at 90mph on the motorway was a doddle and felt like you were standing still. Jane was having fun with the stereo, playing the different tapes she brought along as I had not yet purchased any of my own.

Soon we were in the countryside, and I was amazed how similar it was to some of the Natal scenes in South Africa. 'You don't have to travel far out of London to reach the countryside. It sure is lovely in Kent; I wouldn't mind staying here, even if it means travelling to London every day.'

'It is called the garden of England, and you're right; many people commute to London daily, even as far out as Folkestone. I even tried it for a while but found I was too tired to go out at night with friends. You seem to spend your whole life working and commuting. Therefore, I found a room with the idea of going home every weekend, but lately, it has become once a month as I made more friends in London.'

The trip took about two hours. We were met by Mr and Mrs Fisher, who were both in their late fifties and lived in a lovely big house on Sandgate Road. Her brothers were not up yet; apparently, they had a late night and, being Saturday, they were having a lie-in.

We were scarcely sitting down for breakfast when a noticeably worse for wear young man stumbled into the kitchen wearing only a pair of boxer shorts. Mrs Fisher shouted, 'Graham, go back upstairs, wash your face, and get dressed. We have visitors.'

Graham replied, 'Aah, how is one supposed to sleep with that smell of bacon?' Mrs Fisher shoved her chair back and stood up slightly threateningly. Graham responded, 'Okay, I'm going.' He staggered out of the room.

Sitting down again, Mrs Fisher remarked, 'These boys, they will never grow up.'

After breakfast, Mr Fisher and I retired to the lounge with a cup of tea and a cigarette. He was telling me all the points to be wary of at auction. The most important being: don't buy a property unless you have inspected it or to use a surveyor if you are not sure. Always study the legal pack before you make a bid. It is also wise to ask an estate agent what the value of the property after renovations would be. He insisted that if I followed these basic rules that investing in property was a sound idea, both for resale and the letting market.

Mr Fisher had also found two properties advertised for auction the following week. Graham and George were now dressed and insisted that they would come with me to inspect the properties and give me a rough idea of renovation cost. We decided to see the houses after lunch, Mr Fisher was to arrange for collection of the keys.

Jane took me for a walk on the promenade and to see the old Grand Hotel where the royals used to spend their holidays. The architecture of the old building was indeed grand, and the sea views magnificent. I was impressed with Folkestone, but Jane warned me that thus far, I had only seen the right part of town and that there were extremely run-down areas.

One of the novelties was the Leas lift, initially installed in 1885. It is a funicular railway that carries passengers between the promenade and down to the seafront. The lift operates using water and gravity and controlled from a small cabin at the top of the cliff. It is one of the oldest water lifts in the UK.

After viewing both houses, the consensus was that they were both sound properties but dreadfully outdated. Both needed complete redecoration, new carpets, kitchens, and bathrooms. It seemed that if I could get them around the guide price, it would allow ample opportunity for renovation while giving a reasonable profit if I was to resell. As I was only looking at the rental market, they were both considered to be prime candidates as they were near a decent school. They also promised a reasonable return that would be big enough to cover a mortgage.

They had scheduled the auction for the following Wednesday. Mr Fisher volunteered to attend on my behalf, saving me the trip down. I, however, thought that this would be my first auction. Therefore I wanted to attend in person and suggested we go together. Jane told me that she would also like to be there and would try to take the day off. Her two brothers were excited, stating that they could complete the work in three to four weeks, barring any hidden problems.

That afternoon on our way back to London, Jane conceded, 'You know, if you are going to buy more houses for the letting market it would not be a bad idea for me to take a course in interior design. I had always liked planning the colour schemes of rooms and the layout of kitchens.'

'Why not? If that's what you like doing, it would be a great help as I intend to build up a portfolio of houses. What's more, I would be happy to pay for your course. Why don't you enrol straight away and we can use these two properties for you to experiment on with the help of the estate agents.'

Jane could not contain her excitement. 'Does this mean I can choose the kitchen, the bathroom, the flooring, and all the wall colours?'

'Sure, as long as you remain within our budget and you don't get too carried away with the colours and put off the tenants. Remember, this is a business and profits must be made.'

'Don't worry, I won't be too daring at first and will listen to advise. What a lovely thought, everything will be done to my approval. My brothers will be dumbfounded. I can see their faces now, taking instructions from me, their baby sister. Ooh, I can't wait.'

'Your brothers will be enormously proud of you and I am sure they will help you in deciding what fixtures are best suited for the individual properties.'

After dropping Jane off, I returned to my apartment to find the phone ringing persistently. It was Detective Ashton. 'Come for a beer; I have some news regarding Mr Mthetwa.'

He suggested a pub not far from where I lived, and we arranged to meet in half an hour. The pub was called The Three Anchors, and it was a white two-story building with a car park on the left and wooden tables and chairs in front. On the right, it had a children's play area. A waist-high concrete wall protected the whole setup.

After parking my car in one of the many parking slots, I entered the pub. The main room had only a large bar with several tables and chairs. The pool table and dartboard were in a separate room. I found the layout pleasing and thought that this could with no trouble become my local.

I spotted Mike, now in more casual attire, standing at the bar and joined him. 'Hello, James, what would you have?'

'Hi, Mike, a lager for me, I'm driving.' The barman immediately presented me with a lager beer. What prompt service, I thought, I will come here again.

'Well, let's hear it. Have you arrested Mr Mthetwa?'

'No such luck. I don't know how we are going to pin Sarah's murder on him. But he is involved in all sorts of illegal activities. We think he is a primary dealer in all types of class A drugs and maybe we can get him for that.

If we can prove that he is dealing with drugs, the authorities will automatically cancel his visa as he would become an undesirable visitor to this country.'

'Can't you raid his house?'

'James, to raid his house we need a warrant. To get a warrant, we need to convince a judge that we have a strong suspicion that there are drugs on the premises. The truth is these drug dealers are not stupid. Once they receive a new supply, immediately it is distributed amongst their runners who essentially sell the drugs to the users, they do this to prevent the collapse of the whole organisation when someone gets caught. If they have to hold a large stash of drugs, they hide it somewhere safe, away from where any of them live.'

'That's not good enough, Mike. I want him punished for Sarah's murder. We will have to flush him out somehow. I have bought a flash car to try and annoy him into thinking I am spending his diamond money. Maybe he will do something stupid without the goons he's hiding behind.'

'James, I don't think you realise how dangerous your Mr Mthetwa is. He does not seem to have any value for human life. I must stress that you should be extremely careful and if anything happens, contact me immediately. Don't act on your own as it might be illegal and, certainly, dangerous. Now, let's go and examine this flash car of yours.'

Downing our beers, Mike followed me out to the car park. 'A Pagoda top Merc!' he exclaimed. 'This will stir up things with Mthetwa.'

'It's only second hand, but I hope it will do the trick,' I answered modestly.

Watching Mike getting in behind the steering wheel of my car to inspect the interior, I was suddenly overwhelmed with trepidation. I wished my dad were here as I had no idea what to do next. He was always wise.

I don't think I was scared of a physical confrontation with Mthetwa, but these guys used knives and guns, which was entirely out of my league. Mike's warnings did not ease my thoughts either. Maybe it would be a good idea to temporarily move out of my apartment as I felt vulnerable there on my own.

Getting out of the car, Mike remarked, 'This sure is a lovely car. It's bound to make anyone envious. Even the pope will be jealous.'

'That's what worries me. Do you think I should find alternative accommodation for a month or two? I feel vulnerable in the apartment on my own. I thought maybe I should try this pub if they do bed and breakfast.'

Mikes face lit up. 'You know, if you can afford it, I think that is a good idea, I don't think Mthetwa will try anything here, it is too public. Come, let's go and talk to Terry. I know him fairly well, and am sure I can get you a good deal.'

We discussed the situation with Terry, the pub's landlord, who was especially pleased to help. I took the room for one month, with an option to extend to two months. Terry explained he did not want permanent lodgers for extended periods as he liked to have a few rooms always available for when his customers had too much to drink and could not drive home.

CHAPTER TWENTY-ONE

I moved in that same evening and had a pleasant night's sleep. The next morning, I returned to my apartment to make a few phone calls, letting everyone know where to contact me. Jane thought staying at the pub was an excellent idea. Although I knew that it was going to be a bit difficult doing the flowers without a phone, I must admit I was feeling a lot more relaxed, and I even had some thoughts about Mr Mthetwa.

First, I needed to get close to him and to do that I needed the help of Mr Ahman. Fortunately, he was still at the Savoy and agreed to see me that afternoon at the office where Jane worked.

Jane was all smiles and excited on my arrival, eagerly wanting to know if it would now be safe for her to visit me at the pub as her boarding house was not suitable for visitors. We agreed to meet there that evening after work. I think she thought I was somewhat aloof, but the truth was that I was incredibly nervous in asking Mr Ahman for help.

Jane informed me that Mr Ahman was in his office and waiting to see me. I felt like I was going for a job interview as I walked down the passage to his office.

Only, he greeted me with a friendly smile and a handshake.

'Well, James, it's good to see you, but I am intrigued. What can I do to help?'

'I had a meeting with Mike Ashton yesterday; he explained that it would be exceedingly difficult to prosecute Mr Mthetwa for Sarah's murder. My thoughts were to flush him out into making some mistake. Therefore, the car I bought to provoke him. Mike warned me how dangerous these guys can be and that they are also most likely involved in drug dealing. I then took a room at the local pub for a month or two as I felt vulnerable alone in my apartment. This morning it occurred to me that the only way to ever lay a trap for Mr Mthetwa was to get close to him. At the moment I have no chance as the only interest Mr Mthetwa had in me was to punish me for taking his diamonds.

What I had in mind is if it could be made known to all that I represent you here in London while you are home in Switzerland. I could then concoct some scheme to try and entrap Mr Mthetwa.

You have dealings in many different fields, and if the word is out that I am your agent or representative, I soon will become exceedingly useful to Mr Mthetwa. I will report to you every day on all customers' enquiries and follow your instructions on how to deal with them explicitly. I do not expect any payment whatsoever, even if there are expenses. I think two months is all I need and promise not to divulge any information or contacts to anyone.'

Mr Ahman asked me to leave him for half an hour to give him time to consider my proposition. I stated I would go and sit with Jane, and that he simply had to call when he was ready.

It was not ten minutes later when Jane took a call and told me Mr Ahman was ready to see me. The walk to his office was even worse than last time, and my stomach rumbled continuously.

Mr Ahman asked, 'Would you be willing to come to the office daily?'

'That would be no problem as it would be difficult for me to conduct my flower business from the pub, even if I am winding it down.'

'Well, for some time now, I have been toying with the idea of having a permanent office in London as I am getting old and don't like flying back and forth all the time. I also need more time with my grandchildren. The problem has always been trusting someone to look after things here.

Now, this idea of yours could be an exciting experiment, providing you keep me informed of everything, even your plot to entrap Mr Mthetwa. I have had some dealings with him before, but if he is into drugs, I would be happy to lose him as a customer.

What I propose, you do your thing for a month or two using my company as a platform. If after this time we are both satisfied with the setup, I will draw up a contract for us to continue permanently for either a fixed fee or on a commission basis.'

'Thank you, sir, this is more than I expected and will do my best to represent you in an honourable way. At the end of this experiment, I would be delighted to continue permanently.'

We agreed to have some business cards printed, and Mr Ahman promised to have my name added to all his correspondence as his London representative. He also instructed Jane that I would occupy his office and that she should direct all calls to me.

Throughout the day, Mr Ahman showed me all the deals he was currently working on and a list of all his contacts. He decided to return to Switzerland that evening as he was homesick. Anyway, he proclaimed, the quicker I got involved, the better for all of us. I only had to telephone if I needed help.

That evening in the pub with Jane, I confessed that I thought I had taken on more than expected. Mr Ahman seemed to be involved in many different deals; it would take me months purely to get my head around it all.

Jane replied, 'Never mind, I am sure you will cope. For me, it is nice merely to have you around all day.'

'It would be some achievement if I could become his representative here permanently. It would be like moving into the first league overnight. Tomorrow, for instance, a guy from Sierra Leone is flying in with some diamonds for sale, and I am supposed to handle it.

Mr Ahman also asked me not to involve Howard in any of his transactions as Howard has a crooked streak, particularly when it came to the intervention board. Creating another problem, I will have to handle as Howard has been a good friend.'

Jane replied with a grin, 'You will have to obey orders if you want to represent Mr Ahman permanently. I am sure he does not want you to stop being friends with Howard or even stop doing deals with him. Simply don't get him involved in Mr Ahman's affairs.'

Terry came over and offered us the use of his private lounge for more privacy. I declined as it would be unfair to his wife and kids if we took over his living room. Jane and I were planning to meet in the pub every day after work and would simply have to get used to public places.

The Three Anchors pub did not have a restaurant but did do pub meals such as fish and chips or pie, chips, peas, and gravy. We settled on the latter. We were pleasantly surprised to find it tasty and filling. It was, however, not the right sort of thing for a healthy lifestyle. Fortunately, Jane frequented an inexpensive café that served more wholesome food.

After our meal, Jane returned to her lodgings, and I had a whisky and retired to my room as the next day would be challenging for me, negotiating the purchase of diamonds from Sierra Leone.

I arrived at the office the next morning at 9 am and was delighted that Mr Ahman's diamond expert was there waiting for me. He introduced himself as Jan van der Geest. I told him my knowledge of diamonds was limited, and I would be relying on him to help make this transaction successful for Mr Ahman. He assured me of his support and added that he does many such deals with Mr Ahman, and I need not be concerned; all would go smoothly.

Mr Ahman phoned and also assured me not to be concerned. He realised it was large sums of money and naturally I would be worried, but that I should purely treat it as figures. I wouldn't even see the money. The first thing I should do is photograph the diamonds and then count them together with whoever delivers them. Then issue a receipt signed by the delivery person, myself, and Mr. van der Geest.

Jan would then check the diamonds and privately give Mr Ahman a value. Mr Ahman would then phone me and tell me what to offer. If he accepted the price, the three of us would go to the bank to hand over the diamonds to the manager for safekeeping, again making sure to get a receipt. The manager will then pay the agreed amount into the seller's bank account—end of the story.

Mr Ahman made it sound simple, but I knew that if anything went wrong, I would be the one responsible. I thought that I should be especially careful. I excused myself and walked over to reception to clear my head and to remind Jane that we had an auction to attend the following day.

'I know, was about to remind you but thought not to bother you with all that you have on your plate today.'

We hardly started talking when two African men entered, requesting to see Mr Ahman. I introduced myself and explained that Mr Ahman was not available and that I would deal with them. They introduced themselves: the elderly gentleman was Mr Dhlamini and the younger chap Paul Nwosa.

I escorted them to my office, where I introduced them to Mr. van der Geest as our diamond expert. I explained to them the procedure as stipulated by Mr Ahman and, if they agreed, we could start.

Mr Nwosa took out a large envelope from his briefcase and deposited the contents on a black cloth Mr. van der Geest had placed on my desk. I immediately photographed the diamonds, and together we counted them. There were forty-six stones. We all agreed, and I made a receipt signed by all four of us.

Mr. van der Geest then started examining them one by one, noting figures on an A4 pad on the desk. These diamonds did not look the same as the ones I sold Mr Ahman, but a lot of them were more substantial. Looking at them, I thought it was a good thing that I didn't have to decide on their value, as to me they seemed entirely worthless and uninteresting; they did not seem to have any sparkle.

Anyway, after about an hour, Mr. van der Geest excused himself for a few minutes, and on his return, my phone rang; it was Mr Ahman. He told me to offer them £300,000. I conveyed the offer to Paul and Mr Dhlamini, who, shaking their heads, refused and stated that the least they would take is £400,000. I discussed this with Mr Ahman, who asserted he would pay that, but I should see if I could get away with paying a bit less.

I explained to Paul and Mr Dhlamini that Mr Ahman felt that £300,000 was what they were worth, but as he wanted to continue doing business with them, he was willing to increase the offer to £325,000.

There was a lot of discussion between the two in a foreign language unknown to me. Eventually, Paul countered that £330,000 would make them happy. Mr Ahman agreed and advised he would contact the bank immediately.

Mr. van der Geest folded up the black cloth with diamonds inside and placed it in his briefcase and locked it. Then he handed it over to Paul to carry to the bank. He handed the key to me, and the four of us marched over to a branch of Credit Suisse, Mr Ahman's bank here in London.

The manager was expecting us. We recounted the stones, found that there were still forty-six of them, and Mr. van der Geest was happy that they were the same stones. The manager then gave us a receipt and asked the Africans the details of the bank account they would like the money deposited. He gave them a receipt proving that he had done it.

We bade them farewell and returned to the office. I immediately phoned Mr Ahman, who was pleased with the price we paid and congratulated me on a successful transaction.

Relieved, I declared to Mr. van der Geest, 'Jan, I'm pleased that's over. How about a spot of lunch? I don't think I will do any more work this afternoon.'

'That will be lovely. I hope you realise why this transaction went off this easily. I am positive these are stolen diamonds, or at least they did not pay or work for them,' Jan replied.

'Why do you think that?'

'Well, firstly, they accepted a price well below the market value. If they were the owners, we would still be arguing about the price. Secondly, they seemed to agree with everything we put to them. Actual owners would be more possessive and careful, especially dealing with an unknown person.'

Taken aback, I replied, 'We won't get into any trouble with the police I hope?'

With a wide grin on his face, Jan explained, 'No chance. Mr Ahman was not born yesterday. They are almost certainly being cutting the diamonds as we speak, making them incredibly difficult to identify. I saw a security van parked outside the bank, most likely waiting for us to hand over the stones.'

I felt a bit let down; I thought I made an excellent transaction. Being stolen goods, I should have made a lower offer. But how was I to know? It shows that working in this league was incredibly demanding. I would have to be more on my toes in the future.

We went to a restaurant around the corner from the office. Feeling a bit downhearted, I started with a whisky before ordering our meal. Mr. van der Geest reassured me that we paid a reasonable price for the diamonds as he valued them at close to a million pounds and that Mr Ahman would be well pleased.

Feeling a bit more positive after the meal, I returned to the office and greeted Jane. 'Hi, I hope you have done your homework for the auction tomorrow as I have had no time to even think of it. I am relying completely on your judgement.'

'Don't worry, James, it is all taken in hand. My father and brothers will also be there to give advice. I am also starting my course on interior design this evening. Therefore I won't be able to see you after work. But I will be ready for you to pick me up at eight tomorrow morning.' Jane confirmed that a girl from the agency would cover for her and make a note of phone calls and messages.

I called Mr Ahman again, explaining that Mr. van der Geest thought we bought stolen diamonds. If I had known that, I would have offered an even lower price. Mr Ahman confessed that the price I got the diamonds for was reasonable, at least £30,000 less than what he would have paid. He should have told me any diamonds offered for sale in this manner, I must always regard as stolen. It is not for us to verify their origin; we must only take precautions that we don't lose the stones after we paid for them, which is why he arranged for the immediate cutting of the diamonds.

I told Mr Ahman that I would be away the following day to attend the house auction and that Jane would be coming with me; she had a replacement for the day who would take all messages.

Mr Ahman wished me luck, stating that if it looked profitable, he might come in with me in the future as he had trust in my judgement. 'Property,' he declared, 'was always a sound investment.'

That evening, sitting alone at the bar counter of the Three Anchors, I thought to myself, I am only doing this to get closer to Mr Mthetwa. After only day one, I am getting exceedingly involved with Mr Ahman. Where is it going to end? At this rate, I will be too busy to even think of Mr Mthetwa.

After another beer, I again ordered a bar meal, this time fish and chips. I asked Terry if I would be allowed to take a bottle of whisky to my room as I sometimes liked to have a nightcap after I had a bath.

He stated that it was not a problem. Besides, what I do in my room is of no concern to him. 'This is not a hotel. You are more like a private border and that the room is yours to do with what you want. Providing it is within reason. For instance, it would not be acceptable if you sell your whisky to my customers.'

I assured him that it was not my intention. 'I did not want to come downstairs draped in a towel to buy a whisky; it might chase your customers away.'

Terry thought that was funny. 'I can see that your appearance in a towel might be disturbing. You might even start a new trend. God forbids. Have you got some whisky for your room? I can let you have a bottle as long as you replace it.'

'That is extremely kind of you. I will have a bottle of Bell's and replace it tomorrow.'

Armed with my bottle, I excused myself and went upstairs to my room, thinking that it would be nice to be back in my apartment again.

The next morning at 8 AM, I parked outside Jane's lodgings. I had allowed a half hour for her, in case she was not ready. To my surprise, I had hardly opened the car door, and she was leaving her front door. Bless her soul; she was punctual as well as attractive, a rare combination.

I kissed her good morning and opened the car door for her. I tried to compliment her on her punctuality but could not get a word in; she was extremely excited about her interior design class. 'James, this course is the best in the world, and I am lucky that I have this opportunity to put into practice what I am learning. My tutor wants me to photograph each room of the properties, and the whole class is going to use this as a project to learn about interior design. We might even visit the properties.'

'That's not a problem. I am pleased that you are enjoying the course. I am going to leave it all to you as I don't think I will have any time to spend on this project. But remember, we have to buy the houses first.'

Jane, with a big grin on her face, relaxed a bit and allowed me to negotiate the flurry of London morning traffic. Fortunately, most people were driving into London, leaving the exit routes relatively quiet and soon the countryside opened up in front of us.

I told Jane that Mr Ahman wanted to come in with me buying houses for the rental market. It could help spread the risk and will give her brothers a lot of work. It scared me a bit as Mr Ahman has a lot of money, he might soon take over. I was hoping to build up a small portfolio of houses as a steady income, not a multinational business controlling hundreds of homes. Everything Mr Ahman did seemed to be big business.

Jane replied, 'I know what you mean. He has offered you a great opportunity though. However, with it, there is a drawback, like if you're not careful, you will soon be working for him. Whether that is a good idea or not, I don't know. That is for you to decide. All I can say is it's a decision you will have to make soon, as his operation is like a steamroller.'

'Well, let's see how today goes and then I will be in a better position to decide. Have you got a price in mind of what I should bid and what is your estimate of renovation costs?'

'The guide price for each house is five thousand. If you could get them for £4,000 each, leaving a thousand pounds each to modernise them, I think you are safe as you should easily obtain a rental of £50 per month, giving you a yield of more than ten per cent on your capital outlay.'

'You astound me. I did not realise beautiful women could also be brilliant accountants. Do your brothers agree with your renovation costs?'

Jane answered, smiling, 'No, they quoted about £500 each. By replacing the kitchens and bathrooms as well, you will get more rent and a better class of tenant. That's why I had increased the cost to around a thousand pounds per house.'

We arrived at Jane's parents' house, and everyone was excited about the auction. The only one who has been to an auction before was Jane's dad. He insisted that we should agree on the top price we were willing to pay and make sure we didn't bid a penny more.

We all agreed the top price for both houses were not to exceed £8,000. I proclaimed that was all I brought with me, and with that, we proceeded to the auction.

The first house I got for £3,500 but the second house I ended up paying £4,500. There was someone who would not stop bidding, and as I wanted both I could not stop at £4,000. Jane kept on elbowing me in the ribs as we went over the agreed figure and I was pleased to win at £4,500 as I didn't think I would have any ribs left if I went any higher.

After being sternly reprimanded by Jane, who insisted that I should not have paid more than £4000 as there were many houses up for auction, we went to inspect our purchases. I was well pleased. It seemed to me that all the work required was cosmetic, and Jane's brothers agreed that it would not cost a lot to do. I explained that Jane was in charge of the renovations and I was leaving it all up to her.

She was busy taking photos and measuring each room while starting to make sketches on her big drawing pad. I thought she looked professional and was proud of her enthusiasm.

I thanked Mr Fisher for his help and tried to invite the whole family for lunch. Jane, however, wanted to continue with her assessment of the properties and demanded that her brothers remain to quote on the renovations she had in mind.

She stated that London was a long way from Folkestone and she would like to get most of the work organised while she was here. She also wanted to pick up bathroom and kitchen catalogues from the various wholesalers while in Folkestone.

I ended up buying tea and sandwiches for our lunch. After traipsing behind Jane for two hours from room to room and all the local building suppliers, she decided that we could head back to London. We bade everyone farewell and set off, with Jane armed with loads of catalogues and all her sketches' and measurements. She commented, 'Now all I need is 24-hour photo development shop, allowing me to have everything ready for my next design class.'

'You are certainly taking this course seriously.'

'James, this is what I've always wanted to do, restore old, tired houses to life. I want to present such an excellent assignment; you will want to buy more houses.'

'Maybe I should then not look at the buy-to-let market but resell each property after completion. We will have to see how much we can sell these two houses and share the profit. Giving you some income in the event of you wanting to make a career of it. Or maybe I should accept Mr Ahman's offer to buy and sell houses and run my collection of lettings on the side.'

Jane looked concerned. 'I think the latter is safer. Buying and selling properties is a precarious business. You need to know what you're doing genuinely. Buying houses and restoring them for the letting market is a lot safer as it is a long-term investment and allows more room for error.'

'You will have to find more people to work for as I don't think I could afford hundreds of houses. I was thinking more like about ten, and that will not give you a living.'

Jane replied, 'I was not thinking that I could make a living doing interior design only for you. I simply appreciate you allowing me to start. I am treating all the work you give me as part of my learning to become an interior designer while also being able to illustrate them as projects I have done for my portfolio.'

'Well, I will carry on then buying houses and letting you practise your designer talents on them. When you feel ready, I will be happy to help you set up your own business as an interior designer. There must be lots of opportunities here in London alone. Think of all the hotels, hospitals, and office blocks.'

We were engrossed in conversation, that before I knew it, we were approaching London and I had to concentrate on my driving. The first thing to find was a place to develop Jane's photographs, and then we could go for a pub meal at the Three Anchors.

Jane, yawning and stretching beside me, mumbled, 'That would be lovely, but after the meal, I think an early night is on the cards. I did have a wonderful day today and can't wait to put all my ideas into action.'

'Before we have our meal I would like to check if everything is as it should be in my apartment. I bet there is loads of mail waiting for me and the plants need watering.'

We found a 24-hour photo development service for Jane, and then we proceeded to inspect the apartment. Except for the pile of letters, all was well.

On the way to the pub for a meal, Jane asked. 'When are you going to move back into the apartment? It's such a waste, I could have made us a lovely meal, and it is much more comfortable than the pub.'

'I know. Tomorrow I start my campaign to flush these murderers out. I have an appointment with a private investigator who is going to help me.'

After our meal, I took Jane home and returned to the pub to sort through my mail. Most of it was junk and, after a whisky, I retired for the night.

The next morning at the office, our temp girl presented me with a list of ten calls I missed previous day. I noticed one of them was from Mr Cohen wanting to talk to Mr Ahman.

I returned his call without delay and explained to him that I was representing Mr Ahman in his absence and pleased to assist him if it was in my power. Otherwise, I would contact Mr Ahman, and he would fly over immediately.

Mr Cohen affirmed, 'I have another friend who has some Krugerrands for sale. Would the terms and price be the same? How about a meeting at the horse races on Saturday? Mr Ahman might want to come in person. I know he likes the races or else he could give you all the info, and we could go from there. You could tell him that it would be for a large amount.'

'No problem. I will be there and will confirm later whether Mr Ahman will be able to join us.' I phoned Mr Ahman, who immediately agreed to come over for the race meeting. I expected as much as he seemed to be keen; I would not be surprised if he ended up buying a racehorse. Mr Cohen was pleased when I confirmed that Mr Ahman would join us. I could see another celebratory night at the Savoy.

On my way out to see the private investigator, I told Jane that we might be dining at the Savoy on Saturday. Her eyes lit up with excitement and then panic stepped in. 'My hair! Oh, I need a new dress!'

While opening the car door, my mind was filled with great sadness, thinking about how Sarah would have loved this car. It was my duty to make somehow Mr Mthetwa pay for what he did to my Sarah before I could move on.

The private investigator recommended by Howard was Mr Tim Barry. His office was in a somewhat rundown building on Edgware Road. He was on the top floor, and there was no lift. The staircase was in desperate need of a lick of paint. Rubbish littered the floor. I thought to myself that there would be no upfront payments made here.

Tim Barry was a big, 6ft 3 inches tall guy with dark hair and a ready smile. He seemed to be sincere and had a confident look about him. However, it was evident that he was struggling financially as his suit was a typical British Home Store off-the-shelf model, a bit crumpled and, in keeping with the rest of the office, somewhat shabby.

I gave him the list of names and the address in Romford for Zaba Mthetwa and his associates. 'I want these guys harassed by the police. Report them for drug dealing, have them and the premises searched for drugs. Inform the police that they fit the description of the two-people spotted at Sarah's apartment. Report them to various police stations.

Most importantly, you and I must remain anonymous. Oh, Mr Mthetwa likes horse racing. Tell the bookmakers he might be handling counterfeit money.

If possible, it would be advantageous to infiltrate Mr Mthetwa's organisation and tip-off Mike Ashton. It would also be helpful to have a file on each of the gang.

If possible, you can tail them. There would be a bonus if we can pin something criminal on the gang.

I want you to make them wish that they were back in South Africa. I think if you can keep it up for two or three weeks, it will do the trick.

For results, I will pay well. Your first payment will be next Friday, simply state your price. If you feel you can't do what I ask, let me know now. Allowing me to make other arrangements.'

'Mr. Hammond, I am sure I can make life especially miserable for these guys. But tell me, what have they done to deserve this?'

'They murdered my wife-to-be, Sarah, under the instructions of Mr Mthetwa, but Detective Mike Ashton insisted that due to a lack of proof his hands are tied. I intend to make them pay, even if I have to do it myself.'

'If that's the case, James, I am with you all the way. I hope you don't mind me using your first name. I am Tim. Please don't take any notice of the state of the offices and the building. I am out of here as soon as I can afford a new place. I used to work for an agency but decided to go alone, and consequently, I now have to build up clients from scratch.'

I gave Tim all the details about Sarah's death and the full reason why I suspected Mr Mthetwa and his cronies. I arranged to meet him the following Friday afternoon.

With that I left and returned to my office, finding Jane in a happy mood as she sorted out all the photos, she took of the two houses I bought. 'This will excite the class tonight. I can't wait to hear all the different ideas. I want to have some idea of what needs to be done to the houses as I plan to go home on Sunday to instruct my brothers in what work they have to do.'

'I would have liked to come with you on Sunday, but with Mr Ahman here I don't think I can make it. Perhaps it is for the best. I would be interfering with what is ultimately your project. Not that I am not interested, I would appreciate it if you would show me what you have in mind and at what cost, but only when you are ready.'

'Don't worry, James, you will be proud of me on completion of the houses. You wait and see.'

Jane's enthusiasm radiated from her, reassuring me of her total commitment. I could only smile at her excitement.

Reaching my floor, I looked at the doors of the offices I passed and wondered who they represented. I should ask Jane to make me a list of all the businesses that use this building as an address. I would at least know my neighbours. Jane could make one think that she only worked for me, but in reality, she was the receptionist for several companies.

I phoned Detective Ashton and arranged to meet him after work for a beer and a chat in the Three Anchors pub to give him an update. After I finished all the routine calls, I decided to visit my apartment as I was sure it needed a bit of cleaning.

The truth is, I missed the place and wanted to be alone for a while to do some thinking.

The apartment felt dead and empty. It is incredible how eerie a place feels when uninhabited. I immediately switched on all the lights and the TV to try and bring it back to life. After a whisky and going through my mail, I relaxed and again decided that it was a pleasant place to live.

I reluctantly got the vacuum cleaner out and gave the apartment a once over. I couldn't wait to move back; it is nice to have your place. When I do, maybe I should ask Jane to come and live with me. I am sure Sarah wouldn't mind, especially if I had punished the people that harmed her.

I was sure Jane must be thinking there was something wrong with me; it was evident that she wanted me, but in turn, all I have given her is a kiss hello and goodbye. I better move the relationship forward a bit, or soon she will tire of me. I found it difficult, however, to be amorous when Sarah was still foremost in my mind.

Looking at my watch, I realised that it had gone five and that I should get going to the Three Anchors where I was to meet Mike. With my mind drifting in thought, I had lost track of time.

After locking up, I dashed to my car, only to find myself stuck in a severe traffic jam. London at five o'clock is a murder; it would have been quicker to walk. I arrived at the pub at half-past five after what should have been a five-minute journey.

Annoyed with myself for being unreliable at timekeeping, I walked into the pub to find Mike was already on his second beer. 'Hello, James, I was beginning to wonder if you stood me up.'

'Sorry, Mike, I forgot all about the five o'clock traffic. I hope this stupid error on my part is not going to affect any other appointments you may have.'

Mike replied, smiling, 'No, relax. I have finished work for the day, and there is no hurry.'

'Well, in that case, can I buy you a meal or something to make up for the inconvenience I caused? They serve first-rate meals here, providing you are not too fussy. Or maybe you would like to go to a restaurant? I see you are wearing your posh suit and tie.'

'A pub meal would be fine. I was in court again today, therefore the fancy dress. It is a wonder that we solve any cases, we spend to much time in court. I had concluded that unless we get a confession, murder cases are a waste of time as when the barristers become involve there is always some technical problem, like not giving the accused a hanky when he sneezed or something stupid like that.'

'It must be frustrating, doing all that work to find the culprit, only to find some slick lawyer tearing your case apart.'

Mike took a large mouthful of beer and, scowling, replied, 'It is not pleasant I can tell you. Sometimes you feel that you are wasting your time. What I do in most cases is to present the accused with my evidence before the lawyers are involved, showing that we have him bang to rights and then hope he confesses, this works reasonably well with ordinary people. The savvy ones scream lawyer immediately.

Anyway, that's enough of my problems, you wanted to see me, and I think what you wanted to see me about is more important as I am sure it relates to Mr Mthetwa.'

'Let's order something to eat and move to a table in the corner where we can have some privacy.'

Armed with fresh pints of beer, we move to a corner table, where I informed Mike of what I had done employing a private detective. I added that I would give him a copy of all the reports I received, and I would also ask Tim to keep him in the loop if he wished.

Mike replied, 'I think your choice of PI is okay. I know Tim Barry and have found him to be an honest person. What is your ultimate purpose behind this?'

'Well, I have heard that Mr Mthetwa and his gang are in the drug business and I was hoping that Tim could somehow infiltrate them and find out where they are hiding the drugs. I think the easiest way to Mr Mthetwa is through his underlings. If we can trap them, then we might scare them into informing about Sarah's murder.'

'I don't know if that will work, but it is always good to get more lowlifes off the streets. You must realise that you are stirring up a hornets' nest. I should say that you should leave it to the police to handle, but we are too short-staffed for me to promise anything. As long as you keep me informed and you are willing to step aside the minute you have something concrete and let us handle it.'

At that moment Terry arrived with our meal. We both went for the steak pie, peas, chips and gravy, and I must say that it looked scrumptious. Our conversation evaporated as we tucked into our food. After we finished, Mike stated, 'I must compliment Terry on a lovely meal. That was truly excellent. When do you see Tim again?

I look forward to finding out what he has unearthed.'

'I have an appointment with Tim for next Friday morning. Why don't we meet here again on Friday for lunch, maybe Tim can join us? Hopefully, Terry's food is more appealing than your police canteen.'

'That is an excellent idea. You don't want to know what rubbish we have to eat at work. The Met is not like television programmes you watch that make the food always look good.'

Terry came to collect our plates, and we thanked him for the lovely meal. He was pleased, and jokingly he asked, 'Where is that lovely blonde girl of yours?'

'Oh, you mean Jane. She is at college tonight, doing a course on interior design.'

Mike responded, 'I thought you were still yearning for Sarah or is this new girl purely trying to help you get over her?'

'She is my receptionist, but besides that, she is an especially nice girl, and although I still grieve for Sarah, Jane is becoming part of my life, slowly but for sure. I did not want it to happen, but she seems to have the ability to make me like her no matter what mood I am in.'

'I think I understand better now why you have moved in here with Terry. You have done the right thing protecting your friend Jane from becoming involved with these guys you are pursuing. I will see you next Friday at one o'clock. Send Tim my regards, and I hope he can make it.'

With that, Mike left. I wondered if he was married; he never mentioned a wife. I will ask him next time I see him. I had another few beers and went up to my room. Thinking of Jane and smiling at the thought of her tomorrow morning explaining to me all about her class tonight. Tomorrow I must also close down my flower business for good. There were still one or two stragglers selling orchids. I planned to give them the details of my contact in Thailand in case they wanted to import them directly, but I was sure they would not be interested. They didn't seem to be the kind of people to take any risks, spoilt selling on a sale-or-return basis.

Arriving at the office the following morning, Jane was already there with sheets of paper spread out all over her desk. Jumping up to hug me, she exclaimed excitedly, 'We had a fabulous time yesterday at college. My fellow students were green with envy that I had two houses to try my ideas on. They did give me a lot of tips on where to get the nicest kitchens and bathrooms. Anyway, it will all be done well within your budget and will be the smartest in Folkestone. Even the tutor was involved in helping to choose colour schemes to make use of the best sunlight in each room, keeping them light and fresh.'

'You are a sight for sore eyes this early in the morning, not only beautiful but clever as well. I can't wait to see the completed houses.'

Grinning, Jane replied, 'I will be able to give you a completion date on Sunday evening. It won't take long though; my brothers promised me immediate attention, with work starting on Monday.'

I asked Jane for a list of all the companies using the office facilities. It turned out that there were twenty-eight companies on her books but that only Mr

Ahman had a permanent office. The rest used the offices like Howard, only as a front and telephone service if they wanted to use the offices or boardroom for meetings, the company charged by the hour.

Jane never saw most of the companies, only communicating with them by phone. The office building was merely a postal address, situated on Great Portland Street, near great restaurants and hotels, it gave them a prestigious address in London.

The top floor, fully occupied by a development company, who owned the building and employed Jane. They also used the same entrance, and Jane was responsible for announcing their visitors and showing them to a lift that would transport them straight to the development company's private reception.

I headed off to my flower wholesalers to advise them that I was discontinuing importing orchids and, as I thought, none of them was interested in taking over from me.

Returning to the office, I telephone Howard to let him know that I have stopped importing orchids, as it was one of his contact with whom I dealt. He confessed that he is also contemplating quitting as the letter of credit for the butter deal will be cashed next week. He wanted to know where I wanted my commission paid, and I stated that I would fax him my Credit Suisse bank details. I also explained to him why I was working with Mr Ahman and declared that I would always be happy to do deals with him in the future. My apartment would also be available when he comes to London. I hoped that our chat would clear the air as I thought he was a bit peeved that Mr Ahman did not want him to be involved in any of his companies.

Jane decided that we should have a KFC lunch as I was spending far too much eating out. It was enjoyable, the two of us sitting at my desk and munching on chicken pieces and drinking tea. I asked her what she thought of moving in with me at the apartment after I sorted this business with Mr Mthetwa.

'James, it would make sense, but first, we have to see if we are compatible. You have not even thoroughly kissed me, never mind sleeping together. I do think I love you and would like to give it a try.'

I explained to Jane that I felt guilty about Sarah and have been reluctant to make advances as I don't want to endanger her life as well. I had powerful feelings for her and felt guilty and afraid of losing her as I have not been showing my feelings to her.

Jane replied, 'You don't have to worry about losing me. I suspected something like that. Don't worry, finish with your plans with Mr Mthetwa, and then we can start this relationship seriously. Now, what do I wear to the races tomorrow? I have never been before.'

'I am not too sure. You look lovely in most outfits. If the weather is nice, a summer dress, otherwise a two-piece suit, imagine you are going to a smart wedding. I am wearing my light grey suit, in case that gives you some idea. We are meeting Mr Cohen in the member's enclosure; he is a racehorse owner.'

'James, I think I need to go and buy a new dress. My wardrobe is not suited for these occasions, and we are going to the Savoy afterwards.'

'Can you take some time off this afternoon? If you can, I will take you to a shop that I know will have the right clothes for you.'

Jane picked up the phone to see if someone could cover for her for a few hours. She gave me an affirmative nod. I then phoned Mr Cohen and explained things to him. 'Sir, I am planning to bring Jane with us to the races tomorrow. She is the receptionist here, and I am sure you would like her.'

'That's no problem; I thought she sounded like a nice girl.'

'The problem is that she does not know what to wear, and I immediately thought of you. If we come around now, could you help her in selecting the right outfit?'

'I would be delighted, James, I am available all afternoon.'

'Thank you, sir, we will see you shortly.'

With that, I replaced the receiver and turned to Jane. 'You better check your makeup as you are about to be introduced to my family.'

Jane, frowning a bit, spoke out, 'Mr. Cohen is not your family, and what does he know about clothing? He is a racehorse owner.'

'You are right, he is not family, but his brother is my parent's next-door neighbour in South Africa. Me buying you a dress indicates a serious relationship, and I guarantee that everything you do or say will be reported to my mother before the weekend is over. Did I not tell you? Mr Cohen owns a large upmarket ladies' outfitter in Hampstead. Therefore, get yourself ready and let's not keep him waiting too long.'

Jane grabbed her handbag and disappeared into the ladies' toilet for nearly a half-hour, emerging with an unhappy look on her face. 'I simply don't look right. The mirror in the toilets is no good to do your makeup.'

'You look lovely. Come, let's go.'

Driving to the shop was a bit hazardous as Jane continuously manipulated my rear-view mirror to check her appearance. Fortunately, we arrived in one piece, parked up, and entered the shop. Jane was horrified. 'I can't afford any of these brand names on my salary. Let's go somewhere else; this will be embarrassing. I only have £50, and that is not even enough for a deposit.'

'Jane, I am taking you to the races, and I must see that you have the correct outfit. Stop worrying about money and enjoy yourself. Besides, Mr Cohen will give me a big discount as we are nearly related. It works both ways; if he does not give me a discount, I will tell my mother, who in turn will tell his brother, thus bringing shame to the family.'

Mr Cohen appeared and immediately put Jane at ease, saying, 'My wife hates going to the races, everyone talks about what you are wearing, and it makes you feel that if you wear the same outfit more than once they all know. She now only goes on special occasions. She is, however, going to be exceedingly annoyed with me for not telling her about you and James coming. For her, that would have qualified as a special occasion, and she definitely would have joined us.'

Jane replied, 'It would have been nice if she could come. I do need guidance as I don't have a clue as to what to do on these occasions.'

Mr Cohen grinned. 'It is too short notice for her. She's not a beautiful young girl like you who only requires a dress to be ready for an occasion like this. Enough chatting, let's see if there is anything in this store that can complement your beauty.'

With that, he led us straight to what appeared to be the Dior collection. After about an hour of trying on different dresses, Jane ended up with a gorgeous coral body-con dress with matching bronzed fascinator and finished the look off with a cream Chanel handbag and beige Saint Laurent high heels. She looked lovely.

Mr Cohen explained that his driver was picking Mr Ahman up from the airport and that he could pick us up from the apartment around noon. I agreed, not wanting to explain the reason why I was staying at the Three Anchors pub.

On the way back to the office, Jane wanted to know how much the outfit cost. I explained to her that Mr Cohen is giving it to me at the staff price and would let me know later. I advised her not to worry about the price as it is a gift. 'I would recommend that you do not go there for everyday clothes shopping and use it only for special occasions.'

Jane smiled and added, 'I do have two lovely gold bangles to go with the outfit. Now that has saved you a fortune.'

We returned to the office in time to lock up and decided we should head straight to the Three Anchors for a drink. I thought we could pick up a race card each and see if Mr Cohen's horses were running in any races. I also felt that it would be a good idea to buy racing binoculars the next day before we went to the races.

Jane wanted to know why Mr. Cohen's driver was picking us up at the apartment. I explained to her that I thought that after drinks at the races and then drinks at the Savoy, it would be better if she stayed over and didn't drive home. Most of all, I did not feel like explaining to Mr Cohen why I was staying at the Three Anchors pub. 'You see, he got me the apartment.'

We relaxed that evening with our drinks and paged through the race card, even though we did not have a clue what we were doing. I did notice that Mr Cohen's horses, Skydancer and Diablo, were running again. We decided that we would take a hundred pounds each for bets, but that would be our limit.

Closing my book, I admitted this was no good. I would instead ask Mr Cohen, on whom to bet. I was sure he would know better than me. Jane decided she would mark the names she liked and ask Mr Cohen his opinion, stating, 'I once picked the gold cup winner.'

Jane did not want to stay long as she had to do her hair and make all sorts of preparations. We agreed to meet the next morning at ten o'clock at the apartment.

After Jane left, I chatted to Terry for a while, letting slip that I was going to the races. I must have gotten a hundred tips from all the people in the bar. Eventually, I went to my room having concluded that you could pick any horse, as everyone had a different idea as to who would win.

CHAPTER TWENTY-TWO

The following morning, I bought a small pair of binoculars purposely made for horse racing. The idea was to spy on Zaba Mthetwa and his friends. They were sure to be there, and it would be interesting to see if Tim had any influence with the bookmakers. I also bought some wine and champagne in case Jane and I decided to risk it and stay over in the apartment for the night.

At precisely ten o'clock, Jane arrived in her new outfit and hair did to perfection. 'You look stunning. I am sure you will be the most beautiful girl at the races today. If I am a wolf, I will eat you for sure.'

Trying to embrace her, Jane protested, 'Don't touch me; I worked for hours doing my makeup and hair. You can do what you like after the end of the day. But until then, I want to look presentable. Remember, Mr Cohen will report all to your mother.'

Jane was even reluctant to sit down in case she creased her dress. I pointed out that she will have to sit in the car for the journey to Newmarket. Hesitantly, she took a seat on the settee to drink her tea. 'I have never had such a beautiful outfit; it would be a shame to spoil it. I am sure the wealthy people travel in their jeans and then change when they get to the racecourse?'

'Well, as this is your first time at the races, it is a good opportunity to find out if that is indeed what the ladies do. I will ask Mr Cohen if you can sit in the front with the driver. That would be a lot less cramped. I am sure your dress will survive, and you would still look lovely at the end of the day. Simply relax and enjoy the day.'

Jane had hardly finished her tea before she was in the bedroom, checking her makeup, it was going to be a tiring day; I think I will be feeding her champagne at the races to try and help her relax.

Mr Cohen's driver arrived slightly after twelve, fortunately in a spacious Daimler limo that comfortably accommodated all five of us. Mr Ahman and Mr Cohen were both impressed with Jane's appearance and continuously commented on how lovely she looked. Secretly I was pleased that she was sitting in front with the driver as I was feeling a bit over possessive.

Even when we arrived in the members' area at the races, all heads turned in Jane's direction. It was evident that today was her day and she had stolen the show. Mr Cohen bought champagne for all, and in between sips, we eagerly discussed what horses to bet. He stated that his horse Skydancer was a certainty, but with bad odds as it was the favourite. A better proposition was Diablo at ten to one. He felt that this horse could win today. His trainer advised him that Diablo was preforming in practice positively. The rest of the races, he claimed, was anyone's guess and that he had no idea.

I conferred with Jane as to what she would like to bet. She was insistent on spreading the risk and betting ten pounds on the horses she chose in each race, plus twenty pounds on each of Mr Cohen's horses. I decided to only put fifty pounds for a win on Skydancer and Diablo.

Armed with this list, I went to the nearest bookmaker and placed our bets, returning to Jane with a handful of tickets. I don't know what bets Mr Ahman placed, but I was sure that it was most likely in the thousands. Mr Cohen did not bet. He got his kicks by collecting trophies when one of his horses won.

With all the betting out of the way, I now had time to study the crowd to see if I could locate Mr Mthetwa. He was easy to spot as he was holding up several people trying to place a bet with a particular bookmaker. Tim must have done his thing as the bookmaker seemed to be arguing with Zaba about payment.

I shifted to view another bookmaker and, sure enough, there seemed to be a similar problem with one of Mr Mthetwa's associates.

Jane, squeezing my arm for attention, asked, 'What are you grinning at?'

'Nothing truly, I am purely enjoying my purchase of these binoculars. Here, take a look. You can see the horses and jockeys clearly.'

Mr Cohen called us over to the restaurant for something to eat. It was a self-service buffet, and you could eat as much as you like. Jane disclosed that her brothers would love the races and would come only for the food. We both settled on a piece of chicken and more champagne.

Mr Cohen was amused at Jane's selection of horses and tried to teach her how to check the form of the horses, admitting in the end that a lovely name is as good a way to choose a horse as any. If you don't know the owner or the trainer, it was all guesswork.

Two of Jane's selections and naturally both of Mr Cohen's horses won. We were all in high spirits at the end of the meeting. Jane and I each won about £500 in total and were over the moon with delight. Mr Ahman must have won a large sum of money as he invited us all to the Savoy for our evening meal.

On our way back to the car, Jane whispered, 'You know I won more money than what my car is worth today. Can't one do this for a living?'

'Gambling is a mug's game. The only winners are the bookmakers. You need inside information to win. The only reason Mr Cohen invited us today is that he was sure his horses would win. Using the occasion to impress Mr Ahman, he wants to sell him a large number of Krugerrands.

If we were on our own, we would only have had two winners. That means we would only break even for the day. Now that would be a good day. Mostly you are lucky if you have one winner out of seven races. Today with Mr Cohen's help, we had two bankers, and we did not need to bet on the other runners.

To me, spending the day at the races was a good day out. Not because we won but the pleasure of having you by my side.'

Jane was impressed with the reception we received arriving at the Savoy. We were met at the car and escorted to the restaurant where a beautiful table laid for four was awaiting us, done as if they were expecting us.

Jane, hanging on to my arm, whispered, 'You know, I feel like the queen with this lovely outfit, the surroundings, and the attention the *maître d'hôtel* is giving us. Please don't wake me up if this is a dream.'

'It is no dream; it is what a beautiful girl like you deserves. Simply enjoy every moment as this cost loads of money.'

We sat down for more champagne and after that the most delicious meal imaginable. Jane and I decided on lobster thermidor, consisting of a creamy mixture of cooked lobster meat, egg yolks, and cognac, stuffed into a lobster shell.

While waiting for our meal, Jane decided to visit the ladies to freshen up her makeup. The waiters were falling over each other to give her directions. I thought they were planning to carry her.

Mr Ahman asked if it was okay for Jane and I leave after the meal as he and Mr Cohen wanted to discuss the sale of Krugerrands and did not want Jane to get involved. Mr Ahman also asked me to meet him at the Savoy the next morning at nine for breakfast to discuss the week's work.

Mr Cohen advises that his driver was at our disposal and would take us anywhere we wanted to go. I replied home would be excellent as Jane planned to visit her parents in Folkestone the next day and wanted to make an early start.

To finish off our meal, we each had a cognac, and black coffee served in a *demitasse.* After that, I made our excuses and asked our waiter to alert our driver that we were leaving. Mr Cohen came with us to the front door to instruct the driver.

Jane and I had a back seat to ourselves now and spread out like royalty in the luxurious confines of the Daimler. My mind returned to the prospect of spending the rest of the night with Jane alone in the apartment. All sorts of thoughts were flickering through my mind. Is this too soon? What would Sarah think? Is it safe for Jane in the flat?

Taking Jane in my arms, I was about to let her know my fears when she interrupted, 'You know, this has been the best day in all my life, and now I look forward to spending the rest of the night with the man I love the most in the world.'

I was speechless. I could only respond by hugging Jane closer and wondering why I should have all these doubts. Jane seems to be ready. Why can't I simply go with the flow and make this a proper relationship? What was holding me back? Jane is a beautiful girl. Is it perhaps that I have not yet finalised my promises to Sarah? I am sure she won't mind me falling in love with Jane, or will she?

The rest of the trip was in silence, holding each other tightly as if we were scared to be apart. Approaching my apartment, the driver commented that there was a lot of police outside the apartment block. I wasn't alarmed as a few families were living there; we got out, thanking the driver and bidding him goodbye.

The police must have thought we were famous people, with Jane dressed the way she was and us getting out of a Daimler. They all greeted us respectfully and made way for us to enter the apartment building.

It was when we came to my apartment's front door that the alarm bells sounded in my head. The front door was ajar, and the police were coming in and out of my apartment. A sergeant stopped us entering, asking if he could help. I told him that I lived there and asked him what was going on. 'Well, sir,' he stated, 'I am sorry to inform you that there has been a burglary here.'

'What have they taken, and when did this happen?'

He replied, 'Your neighbour saw two African men force their way into your front door at about 7 pm and called the police. I don't think they had time to take much or do a lot of damage as I think your neighbour disturbed them and rewarded for his public-spiritedness with a knife wound. He is not in any danger; an ambulance took him to hospital for a check over. Because of the knife attack, this makes it into a serious incident, and we have to protect the crime scene until forensics have done their job.'

'Could you please inform Detective Inspector Mike Ashton about this? A couple of months ago, in similar circumstances, my girlfriend was murdered, and the two cases may be connected. For the time being, may we go inside to sit down and have a cup of coffee? We will try not to disturb anything.'

The sergeant escorted us to the kitchen. 'You may make yourselves some coffee but don't go into the lounge. That is where the incident occurred.'

I made two black coffees and told Jane she had better go home when she had finished hers; there was no point both of us waiting for Detective Ashton.

Under the circumstance, there was no way that we could spend the night in the apartment. 'I am sorry that such a beautiful day should now end up disastrously. Please forgive me. It was not intentionally.' I gave her a big hug and kissed her. 'Please meet me in the Three Anchors tomorrow afternoon after five when you have returned from Folkestone.'

After Jane left, I felt a bit empty inside. Something in the back of my mind, however, was saying that perhaps tonight was not intended, and I should wait until this business with Mr Mthetwa was settled one way or another. I owed it to Sarah to first finish our relationship before I started a new relationship with Jane. Only then could I commit me fully.

After a while, the forensic team and Mike arrived to do their thing. Mike remarked to me, 'You wanted Mthetwa to make a wrong move. Maybe this is it. We have a knife, and it has fingerprints all over it. It seems that the assailants were careless and did not remove it. It could be because they were disturbed by your neighbour.'

'I wonder what their intentions were. They definitely could not still be looking for diamonds?' I commented while pouring Mike a coffee.

Mike replied, 'No, I think this time they were after your skull. It was a wise decision to move to a pub. It would be interesting to hear what Tim your PI has been doing to annoy them this much. You will have to be extra careful from now on. You no doubt are staying at the pub tonight. If you like, I can contact an emergency locksmith to come and secure your front door.'

'Yes, please,' I replied to Mike. 'I was wondering if I should stay here all night to guard my apartment.'

We were interrupted by the sergeant; he informed us that the neighbour had returned from the hospital and was ready to answer questions. As Mike was keen to ask him a few questions, I asked if I could come with him as I needed to thank him for what he had done.

My neighbour was a Mr John Murray; I thanked him and insisted that if he had any expenses resulting from his brave actions, I would be more than happy to pay, even for time lost from work while he is recovering.

Mike interrupted, 'You two can sort out your domestics later. What I need to know now is what happened.'

John Murray explained that he was coming back from the pub, and as he stepped out of the lift, he noticed two African guys struggling with my front door. He remained in the shadows of the elevator, watching them force their way into my apartment. Once they were inside, John discreetly followed them into the flat and confronted them in the sitting room, where they were busy destroying my three-piece suite. He tried to stop them, and that is when he was stabbed by one of them. By this time, his wife was also disturbed by all the noise and came to investigate. The two African guys took off, probably frightened by the arrival of reinforcements. He also stated that both he and his wife could identify them.

I thought that this could be the breakthrough I was hoping for, especially if they could link the knife to Sarah's murder. I again thanked John and his wife and allowed him to go and have a lie-down. Mike stated that he would get his sergeant to write out a formal statement for both of us to sign later.

By that time, the forensic team had completed their task and we were free to return to my sitting room. There was not much damage, and after a quick tidy up, it all looked presentable again. The three-piece suite would need replacing, as it had several gashes on the backrest and cushions.

To me, it seemed that their intention was more damage as a warning, instead of an attempt on my life. Theft was not on their minds as they took nothing. Mike agreed with me but warned that I should still be careful and try not to allow myself to follow the same pattern every day.

The locksmith arrived and did a temporary repair for the night; he agreed to meet me at the apartment at noon the next day to do a more permanent job. With the flat secured, we all went our separate ways, and I was soon in a hot bath with a double whisky in the safety of the pub.

CHAPTER TWENTY-THREE

The next morning, I caught the Underground to the Savoy as I did not feel like driving in central London. I met Mr Ahman in the dining room at nine as arranged. I told him what took place the night before and that I felt it was a consequence of the private investigation. Mr Ahman informed that he had a lot of influence with the UK branch of the ANC as they sold their diamonds to him. He would use his power to exert even more pressure on the Mthetwa gang as he was sure that the ANC was not involved in drug distribution. Besides, he would also inform the ANC that, in the future, all their dealings with him should be directed to me as I was his representative in London.

He was especially pleased with how I handled the purchase of the Sierra Leone diamonds; as soon as they were cut and sold, a huge bonus was awaiting me.

Mr Ahman presented me with some business cards. The most important one to me was 'Representative of Zurich Precious Metals.'

The breakfast was again worthy of the Savoy. I had a full English and enjoyed every moment of it. I told

Mr Ahman that Jane was at Folkestone that day, completing the arrangements to modernise the two houses I bought.

He was interested in the buying and selling of houses. I told him that at this stage, I was new to the business and thought it was incredibly risky. What I was doing was buying about ten houses, modernising them, then letting them out to tenants. It was a long-term thing, and I thought of it as my pension.

As it was over a long period and only for letting, it did not matter to me if the renovation cost, plus the price paid at auction, was slightly higher than the market value. Usually, this should not happen, but you have to make allowances for miscalculations, especially when buying at auction.

Mr Ahman stated that he was aware of the risk and understood that I was a bit cautious as I am still new in the business, but as and when I felt more confident, I should let him know. He advised he was keen to start a property business in England.

He also wanted me to send him before, and after photos of the two houses, I had bought. He thought it was advantageous for Jane to take an interior design course, and he was looking forward to seeing the outcome of my venture.

After our meal and chat, Mr Ahman took a taxi to Heathrow Airport for his flight back home to Switzerland. I caught the Underground back to the Three Anchors pub to pick up my car and drive to my apartment for my noon appointment with the locksmith.

While he repaired my front door, I went next door to check on John Murray and to thank him again for his actions. Detective Ashton also arrived at the scene with our statements to sign.

It appeared that although there were plenty of fingerprints, none of them linked with their database of criminals. Mr Murray also went through a book of mugshots of known criminals but could not spot any matching the two intruders he saw. Mike announced he would get the police artist to sketch the two men on Monday.

The rest of the day I spent tidying up the apartment, purely wasting time until 5 pm, when I was to meet Jane. We had only been apart for a short while, and I already felt lost without her by my side.

Later that day we met at the pub and Jane was bubbling with excitement. 'I took my outfit home to show mum and dad. Everyone was impressed, even my brothers. I told them we went in a chauffeur-driven Daimler to Newmarket and that I won five hundred pounds on the races. When I told them that afterwards, we went to the Savoy for a meal to celebrate, they were speechless.'

Terry brought us our drinks, giving Jane time to breathe. 'I showed them my choice of kitchen, bathrooms and colour schemes for all the different rooms in the houses. My dad was impressed and thought that the properties would be upmarket and that we shouldn't struggle to find good tenants. My brothers informed me that they would finish the work in a maximum of two weeks.

Oh, James, I am thrilled and genuinely excited about everything that's happening to me. The only drawback is those people distressing you. I do wish you can get it sorted out. Then we can have a natural relationship. I did not tell my parents what happened at your apartment last night as they would have been horrified. Is your neighbour okay, and what do the police say?'

I explained to Jane what transpired at the apartment and also what Mr Ahman stated, showing her my new business card. 'I am now the official representative in London of Zurich Precious Metals.'

Jane gave me a big kiss and exclaimed with delight, 'I am proud of you, James. I think we should order some champagne to celebrate.' We had a great evening and must have finished at least a bottle of champagne each. Eventually, Jane had to go, and I retired to my room.

CHAPTER TWENTY-FOUR

On Monday morning I phoned Tim and told him what happened, saying that I was sure it was Mr Mthetwa's guys who broke into my apartment. We needed to get fingerprints on the lot of them if that was possible. Detective Inspector Mike Ashton was going to visit with sketches of the two assailants, and it would be nice if Tim could identify them. That would upset Mr Mthetwa.

I asked Tim if he would work with Detective Ashton as he seemed to be a nice guy and wanted to help apprehend the Mthetwa gang. However, he needed to use his discretion as we didn't want to incriminate ourselves. I made plans to see him on Friday but asked that he let me know if anything happened in the meantime.

Jane came into my office with a list of fittings, paint, and carpets she had ordered, stating that only my payment was needed for everything to be delivered the following day.

Together we scrutinised her list but could not find anything she had omitted. Jane confirmed that she also checked it with her brothers. Satisfied that the order was complete, I went to the local wholesaler and paid.

Later that day Tim phoned me, stating Detective Ashton visited him together with sketches of the two burglars and that he was able to identify them as two of Mr Mthetwa's associates. If the fingerprints are positive, and if our eyewitnesses could point them out in an identity parade, they would nail them.

The police were planning to raid the Mthetwa household the following morning at six. They preferred these early morning raids as it caught the suspect on the wrong foot, preferably before they could hide incriminating evidence or even disappear themselves.

That night sleep did not come easy. My mind, cluttered with what-ifs. I was trying to anticipate tomorrow's raid on Mr Mthetwa's house. It would be lovely if they arrest the whole lot of them.

The next day dragged on slowly. It was only after lunch that I received a call from Mike. They arrested two associates of Mr Mthetwa for the stabbing of my neighbour, John Murray. They could not link the stabbing to Sarah's murder, nor did they find any drugs on the premises. The two chaps arrested were identified by Mr Murray and fingerprints were matched with the knife.

Shit, I thought, this was such an opportunity. We will have to find out where they stashed their drugs. Well, I suppose that is at least two down, only four to go. I hoped that the two arrested were the meanest of the lot.

Tim called me later that day with even better news. He thought that he had discovered where they stored their drugs. They were frequently entering a lockup in a small industrial estate. 'This could be it!' he exclaimed. 'I have informed Mike and posted a man to observe the goings-on at this lockup. When we meet on Friday, I should have a full picture of what's going on.'

I tried to keep Jane posted on all developments. I was afraid nothing was penetrating her brain at present; focused entirely on the renovations of the two properties and, on top of that, she had college. Jane had to present all her designs to her tutor for discussion that evening.

After work, I first visited my apartment to check that everything was in order. I was met by John Murray, who was extremely excited that the burglars were already behind bars—praising the police force who, in no uncertain terms, was exemplary. I had to agree with him that, in this instance, they did remarkably well. However, it was thanks to him for intervening in the burglary attempt that made it possible.

I invited him in for a beer. He declined, saying he would love to, but the doctor told him to stay off alcohol while he is on prescription medication, mainly when driving.

I made my excuses and left for the Three Anchors where I took some solace in chatting to Terry over a pint of beer, feeling a bit crestfallen and alone now with Jane in college.

The next morning at work, Jane was excited as she showed me all her plans. Her tutor was impressed with what she had planned for the houses, making me feel proud of her. I asked if we should see the progress this weekend.

'No,' Jane stated, emphatically. 'I am going, but I don't want you near it until it is all completed. I want you to see the end product. Not bits here and there, half done. We can both go the following weekend, then all the work will be done, and you can be stunned by the result.'

Although I was keen to see the progress as this was my first house purchase, I relented and smiled. To me, it felt like my first child growing up, and I only wanted to be part of the process. Secretly I wanted to be in charge and would comment on everything, disrupting the work that they had done.

Frustrated with feeling left out and not able to concentrate on what I was supposed to be doing, I phoned Tim and told him that I was at loose ends and asked if I could help in tailing Mr Mthetwa's gang, or anything else he had in mind.

Tim agreed, and that I should meet him at Romford station in one hour. One of the gang catches the train each day at 1 pm. It would be nice to know where he was going.

At Romford station, Tim handed me a brown folder containing a single sheet of paper with a photograph attached. The man I was to follow was an Amos Sithole.

Tim added, 'I don't think he's dangerous, but don't let him spot you and don't confront him even if you think he's smuggling the crown jewels. We don't want to spook him, please don't give the game away. Only observe and make notes, take photos if possible, and report back to me.'

Tim pointed out Amos Sithole to me to make sure I followed the correct person and then left me to get on with it, dressed in jeans with a dark blue windbreaker and a light brown canvas shoulder bag, which appeared empty. I sat on a bench reading a newspaper, trying to look inconspicuous, but carefully peeping now and then at Mr Sithole to see if he was still there.

The train arrived at 1 pm. Having bought a go-anywhere ticket for the full day, I followed Mr Sithole onto the train and sat a few seats behind him, again reading my newspaper and wondering where we were going. We were on a TFL rail train with a final destination of Liverpool Street. I had to be observant as there were several stops on the way, and he could get up at any moment. I was concerned that he would spot me if he got off at a quiet station, and I tried to follow him.

Luckily, he travelled to Liverpool Street, and since everybody disembarked there, it was easy for me to follow him unnoticed. He decided on the Metropolitan Underground line and, again, I found a seat a few rows behind him. As we approached King's Cross station, he got up, ready to disembark.

I decided that I should leave at the last minute, then he might not notice me, but many people were getting off. I should not have bothered. It made it challenging to tail him in the crowd. If it were not for the fact that he was African, I would have lost him.

Fortunately, because of his colour, I was able to spot him again as he turned left onto St. Pancras Road and continued to Belgrove Street. I managed to take a photo of him entering a building on the left. It was a self-storage depot offering 24-hour access. I took a few pictures of the building and loitered around outside, feeling extremely conspicuous. I had the common sense to walk past the entrance and wait on the far side of the building. I was preventing Mr Sithole not to bump into me on his way back to the station.

About a half an hour later, he re-emerged from the building, his shoulder bag now clearly full. I took a few more photographs and followed him back to King's Cross. This time he did not go to the Underground but to the main concourse of the rail station.

I now had to be especially alert as there were hundreds of people milling about. It did favour me somewhat as I was able to photograph him and three accomplices. He took packages out of his shoulder bag and handed them to his associates. I managed to get this all on film.

Unsure whether I should follow one of these new guys or purely watch and follow Mr Sithole, I went to the nearest phone box and phoned Tim. He affirmed that I must return to his office as I had done my job.

Sitting in the tube on my way to Tim's office, I thought that I somewhat liked this sleuthing. As I climbed the stairs to Tim's office, I again felt that he wouldn't get many clients with all these stairs.

Tim congratulated me on a job well done, confirming my suspicion that I might have found where they stashed their drugs. He asked me to take the photos for development. There was a place nearby that had a 24-hour service. While I handed the pictures in, he would contact Mike and fill him in on what we had accomplished.

After negotiating the stairs once again, I told him, 'I am going to see if there is a spare office in my building. You cannot function like this. You need an office in a decent building with a secretary. Only then will you prosper and get good clients.'

'You are right, James, but I can't afford decent offices yet.'

'Maybe you need a partner or, what do you call it, an associate?'

Tim replied, 'Where am I going to find an associate? There is a lot of hard work and sometimes danger involved. Not many people are interested in this sort of work. If they like this type of work, they will join the police, at least then one is protected by the law, and they have a large workforce.'

'I enjoyed what I did this morning. Maybe after my troubles, I would be interested. For the time being, I will check out the cost of decent offices. You cannot carry on from here; no self-respecting client will even visit you here, never mind giving you work. The only reason that I came here is that Howard recommended you and Mike think you are okay.'

That evening Jane was not in college, and we had a pub meal and several drinks together. The conversation still revolved around interior decorating. Jane was excited by the whole project she could hardly contain herself.

I am sure if I proclaimed 'I love you', she would have asked what colour we should make that or what would be the best shape. All I could do was to humour her and be glad that she was happy.

I could see that we would have to visit another auction soon to buy the next house for her to renovate or else she would be lost, not knowing what to do with her time.

Keeping Jane busy at this stage was vital to me. If she were bored, she would start worrying about our relationship and my antics with Mr Mthetwa's gang.

That night after Jane had left for home, I went up to my room, poured myself a double whisky and analysed what had happened that day. The lockup in Romford that we hoped might be where they stashed the drugs, turned out to be a store for products that were sold in Romford by a door-to-door sales team, controlled by Mr Mthetwa, but all legal and above board. The self-storage unit in King's Cross might be the one. We would have to wait and see.

My mind wandered to the subject of private investigation. I might like doing that. Not all the work would be dangerous. Indeed most of the time, one would investigate insurance fraud and industrial espionage. I could easily fit that in with Mr Ahman's work. Besides, it was a more realistic career as these deals of Mr Ahman or Howard were not a daily thing. More like horse racing.

With all these thoughts going through my mind, I ended up having a restless night. The next morning, I was up early, had my breakfast, and collected the photographs I handed in the previous day.

I called Mike to let him know that I had the photographs for him to see if he could match them with any known criminals. He confirmed that Tim had discussed the operation with him and that he was organising a raid on the self-storage unit as we spoke but that it would be nice if they could identify some of the culprits beforehand. He asked me to put the kettle on; he was on his way.

Mike arrived and studied the photos. He was pleased and stated that you could see that Mr Sithole went into the self-storage unit with an empty shoulder bag and came out with his bag full. The photos of his accomplices were also remarkably clear and hopefully matched someone known to them. He exclaimed that he hoped that they hit the jackpot and find the drugs as it would please his superiors. Getting the drugs off the streets was extremely important, and he thanked us for the information.

I asked Mike for his opinion about me becoming an associate of Tim, with better office facilities and offering a more professional service. Mike replied, 'I think it is a good idea, especially if you work with the police. The problem with most PIs is that they become too secretive, supposedly protecting their clients and thus fall out with the police. Once this has happened, it is difficult for the police to assist them when they are needed. We dislike most PIs for this reason, but thus far, Tim has been especially cooperative, and we are willing to help where possible. I would say, go for it. I could introduce you to several companies who require help.'

With that, Mike left, saying he would phone me later that day to let me know if the storage unit was the jackpot.

I phoned Tim to tell him about my meeting with Mike and the raid he was planning on the self-storage unit later that day. I asked him if he needed any more help. He thought it was best to wait for the result of the raid, as I was seeing him on Friday morning, we could then discuss with what else I can help. He pointed out that if the search were successful, there would only be three people left in Mr Mthetwa's gang.

After that, I went through to Jane's office and asked if she could find out if we could take another office on a full-time basis and how much would it cost. I also asked her if she realised that she should be looking to see if any more houses were coming up for auction.

Jane replied, grinning at me, 'I have been thinking of that but did not want to rush you. I thought I would wait until these two are ready. I have discussed it with a letting agent in Folkestone, who told me that there would be no trouble in finding suitable tenants for both properties. Indeed, she has two families ready to take immediate occupation. Therefore, if you want me to find you the next auction, I am ready.'

I told Jane to set up an appointment for the next auction and to ask her brothers to check out the houses on offer, but stipulated, 'I would like to at least inspect these two houses before you let them out.'

Jane assured me that she wouldn't let anyone move in until I have seen the finished houses.

'Okay, it is time for lunch. I have a few things I would like to discuss with you.'

Knowing it was her college evening, I decided we should go to a local restaurant, to let her have a proper meal as she would miss her evening meal.

Over our lunch, I explained to her about my idea of working with Tim, which is why I would need another office.

Jane responded, 'You want to be a private investigator, isn't that a dangerous job?'

'No,' I responded. 'It is insurance investigation, divorce investigation and industrial investigation. Anything dangerous, you involve the police.'

Jane reached out, squeezing my hand. 'Please remember that. I don't want you to get involved in anything dangerous.'

That afternoon was dreadfully dull; I was unable to concentrate on anything, and eagerly awaited Mike's call to update me on their raid.

At half-past four, he phoned, saying only, 'Success. See you at the Three Anchors after five.' I supposed he did not want to discuss police business with me over the phone.

I kissed Jane goodbye and headed to the Three Anchor pub. In my excitement, I arrived a bit early and had to nurse a beer for at least half an hour before Mike and Tim strolled in.

I ordered a round, and we found a secluded table in the corner. Both Mike and Tim were grinning like Cheshire cats. 'Come on, spill the beans. I can't stand the pleased look on your faces for much longer.'

Mike replied, smiling broadly, 'This was the best raid in my whole career that I have undertaken. The self-storage unit was jam-packed with cocaine. They are still busy accessing the total value of the haul.

To top it all off, we managed to arrest five people, and more charges might follow for the staff of the self-storage company. We have applied for a warrant to search for drugs in all the units. We are sure that they were at least aware of what was going on under their roof.'

Tim chipped in, 'Now there are only two people left in Mr Mthetwa's gang.'

Mike continued, 'You know that this will probably guarantee my promotion to Chief Inspector, and it is all thanks to you guys for alerting me to the activities of these criminals. I still don't see how we are going to implicate Mr Mthetwa, though. Under interrogation, no one has even let slip his name, although we know that he must be involved as the guys we arrested cannot fund such a large quantity of drugs. He must be furious.'

For some unknown reason, probably as they were to collect a large sum of money, Mr Sithole accompanied Amos Zuma to the self-storage units. They were allowed to enter, and then the police swooped on them.

At the same time, with the aid of my photographs, the second team of police arrested three more accomplices on the concourse of King's Cross station. Loaded with cash, and each one had enough cocaine to be classified as dealers.

Mike further stated that if we are of such assistance to the police in future, he will go out of his way to support us as a private investigation agency.

I notice that our beer glasses were nearly empty and offered, 'This calls for another round.' I signalled to Terry behind the bar.

It was excellent news, but the original problem of trapping Mr Mthetwa still existed. I bet he was not a happy bunny. Most of his crew arrested and all of his drugs confiscated. It would be nice to know what is going through his mind at this moment.

Going on Mike and Tim's excitement, it seemed that our new private investigation agency had the green light and could become a reality. I played with the name Barry, Hammond and Associates in my mind and liked the sound of it.

After a joyous evening, Mike and Tim left with the plan to meet for drinks again Friday at five. Tim reminded me that we were to meet on Friday morning at his office where he would give me a full update on Mr Mthetwa. We could then also discuss the agency.

The following morning, I phoned Mr Ahman and told him about the raid on the self-storage units. I also asked him what he thought about the idea of me forming an agency with Tim, the private investigator. He replied that if I didn't think it would interfere with his work, he could see no reason why I could not combine the two. With the recommendation of the police, it would give us a certain amount of prestige, which would be advantageous for all of us.

He also declared that he would phone the ANC immediately to let them know that he would not deal with them if they were involved in drug trafficking. He thought this would bring even more pressure down on Mr Mthetwa as the ANC had previously stated that they don't approve of drug dealing. They might also cut all ties with Mr Mthetwa.

Jane came hurrying into the office, stating that her boss had agreed that I could have the office next door and that we could use the boardroom on an hourly basis. I decided to this immediately. We would now have two offices and a room where we could meet new clients, with Jane answering the telephone and making appointments. It could not be a better arrangement, and I was anxious to tell Tim.

Full of excitement, she informed me that three houses were coming up for auction in Folkestone the following Wednesday. I replied, 'I would like to see the first two out for rent before I spend money on more houses. From now on I think we should only buy one house at a time.'

Jane looked sombre, I thought, as a proper businesswoman. 'You can inspect both houses on Wednesday before the auction. We will also see the letting agent who will give you details of the tenants she has in mind. I agree with you that you should only do one house at a time unless the houses go for bargain prices at auction.'

It looked to me like as all systems go. If there is an auction for three houses, to get a bargain you need to bid on all three. The only problem is that you might end up getting all three.

As this was not a college night for Jane, we went to a proper restaurant for our evening meal. At around nine that evening, I dropped Jane off at her lodgings and returned to the Three Anchors pub. As I entered the car park, I had this weird sensation to take care, as if someone was warning me of coming trouble.

I got out of the car and moved to the rear, which saved my life. A loud gunshot rang out, shattering the outside door rearview mirror. A dark figure jumped into a navy blue or black car and sped away.

In a bad temper, I got into my car and, instead of following them, I drove directly to Zaba Mthetwa's house in Romford, disregarding all speed limits and not caring if I pick up a speeding ticket.

On arrival, the place was in darkness, with no car in the drive. I parked nearby but out of sight and walked back to the house. Fuming that this man could do as he liked but I have to take care, even having to stay in a pub for safety. It has to stop; it should be him that is hiding as he is the murderer.

I sneaked into the drive and waited, hiding behind a fir tree and waiting for his return. It was about fifteen minutes later that his car entered the drive. There were two of them; he was driving. I allowed him to get out of his car, then not caring whether he had a gun or not. I walked up to him and kicked him between the legs as hard as I could. As he was bending down in agony, I hit him in the face with all the force I could generate. I must have penetrated his skin; blood was all over his face. Because my action was out of the blue, he did not even try to defend himself. He lay on the ground whimpering, with his hands still clutching his groin.

His mate was taken by surprised. He simply ran away. I searched Zaba, found the gun and opened the magazine, revealing the bullets, which I emptied and then dumped the shells onto him. I told him that I was compiling a file, large enough to imprison him for life.

I then returned to my car and drove back to my apartment. It was the only place I could think of to make a private phone call. I phoned Mike, explaining everything that took place.

Mike told me that my actions were illegal. I should have reported the shooting incident directly to the police and allowed them to handle Mr Mthetwa. I shouldn't have taken matters into my hands. Now, if I report the shooting, I would get into trouble for assaulting Mr Mthetwa. Hopefully, he wouldn't bring charges against me.

Mike conceded putting Mr Mthetwa in his place might be a good thing. However, I had better not let on that I discussed this with him as he would have to report it; this was all strictly off the record.

I decided to spend the night in the apartment as I was now absolutely shattered. I poured a double whisky and had a relaxing bath, nursing the hand with which I hit Zaba.

The next morning, I took my car to the same dealer I bought it from, who fortunately had a matching rearview mirror and fitted it for me straight away. I drove to the office, greeted Jane and then proceeded to Tim's office via the Underground.

I told Tim about my antics of the previous night and settled his bill. After that, we agreed to form a partnership, with him moving into the new offices immediately. We also decided to move his phone number to the new premises as it would be good to have a telephone number that did not route via the switchboard. His old office was on a monthly rental basis, giving him access for the rest of the month.

As the office came furnished, he was in no hurry to remove all his files. He only needed his word processor and desk in the new offices. We agreed that he and his wife would be on a token salary until such a time when the business could afford decent wages for all of us. Tim's wife came in three mornings a week to do all the typing and invoicing. She was happy to work out of Tim's office and also helped Tim to keep the offices clean.

Tim's wife was Sandra, and she was a petite and attractive girl with a friendly personality. I could tell she was glad of the move as she immediately suggested sending a mailshot to all of his old clients as well as any businesses, we could think of that might require our services, such as lawyers and insurance companies.

Tim and Sandra moved in the same day. They were exceptionally impressed by the size of the office and the plush boardroom at our disposal for meetings. Jane showed them all the facilities. I heard Sandra say to Tim, 'The toilets here are better than your old office. There is even a place where I can check my makeup.'

That afternoon we had a meeting with Mike at the pub. Jane went to Folkestone to see if the houses were ready for inspection the following Wednesday. Mike asked if he could have some of our mailshot letters as he knew a few people who would be interested in our services.

No one mentioned the shooting incident, which I took as an indication that it not reported and we should not discuss it in Mike's presence. Instead, Mike could not stop talking about the successful raid that they had at the King's Cross self-storage company. He was sure that, in time, one of the captured dealers would spill the beans and implicate Mr Mthetwa. He was in no doubt that he was behind and controlling the whole outfit.

Tim had a file with him on the only other member of the gang still left. He was a Mr Leonard Ndlovu, 35 years old; he did not know what his immigration status was. Mike took the file to check if he was known to the police. Tim had a lot of contacts as he used to be employed by MI5 until a year ago. I asked, 'Were you a spy, then?'

Tim replied that MI5, the Security service, is the United Kingdom's domestic counter-intelligence and security agency and should not be confused with MI6, the secret intelligence agency.

'I gave that up when I married Sandra as I thought that I would be at home more as we planned to start a family. I then joined a private detective agency. I could not settle, as my function was as an office clerk, I wanted to get out and do fieldwork.

I left them a few months ago and tried on my own, but as you can see, I was underfunded, and clients did not take me seriously. I think my biggest downfall is that I am not much of a businessman and cannot market the business successfully.'

'Well,' I confessed, 'I am not much of a businessman either, but I think between the two of us we should be able to get the ball rolling.'

Mike interrupted, 'There is such a demand for private investigators, within a month or two you will have that much work, you will be struggling to cope. The big secret is to keep your nose clean and don't upset any authorities.'

Mike and Tim departed, and I faced a quiet weekend on my own until meeting Jane on Sunday evening for a meal and a review of her weekend.

On Sunday at 5 pm, Jane entered the pub full of excitement and pleased with herself, stating that her brothers would complete the two houses before Wednesday. The carpets were being fitted on Monday, and that would be it; they would be ready for tenants. The letting agent was also pleased with the standard of the finish and would meet us there on Wednesday with details of the tenants. She also confirmed our appointment at the auction and affirmed she would give me the details of the three houses on which we were to bid.

Taking her hands in mine and smiling at her excitement, I declared, 'I am sure you have done a marvellous job. I can't wait to see the results on Wednesday. You are no doubt going to take loads of photos for your tutor and classmates.'

'Certainly,' Jane replied. 'I can't wait to see their faces. I am proud of what I have achieved.' We had a pub meal consisting of fish and chips and a few glasses of wine before retiring for the night.

The following day not a lot happened, other than helping Tim and Sandra find their feet in the new office, like getting the phone number transferred. That evening Tim and I went to his old office to collect the last of his files, only to find two African men leaving his office. The one was Mthetwa, with folders in his hand.

Tim shouted, 'Quick, stop him! He is heading for the fire escape; I will catch the other one.'

Mr Mthetwa fumbled with the fire escape door and, as he opened it, I dived at him like in a rugby tackle. My weight and momentum forced him to fall against the safety railings of the fire escape.

Unfortunately, like the rest of the building, the top safety rail of the fire escape was loose and rusty. It came undone, and Mr Mthetwa fell six stories to the ground, bouncing on the lower sections of the fire escape on the way down.

For a moment I stood there dumbfounded until Tim shouted, 'I will call the police and an ambulance!'

He got distracted by all the noise that he had forgotten about the other intruder. While Tim made his phone call, I carefully climbed down the fire escape. It was in such a state, making me wonder what would have happened if there was a fire.

When I reached Mr Mthetwa, I felt for a pulse but could find none. Tim joined me after a while, stating that the emergency services, including Mike, were on their way.

I told him I thought they would be a bit late since Mr Mthetwa was dead. The ambulance and the police arrived at the same time, confirming my findings. The police taped the area and commented that we needed to wait for forensics and the pathologist.

The constable was in the process of taking my statement when Mike arrived. My story to the police was a bit different; I stated that I chased Mr Mthetwa to the fire escape, where he slipped and fell against the fire escape railing. Which gave away, and he tumbled down to the ground.

Tim told Mike that the other intruder was still hiding in the building. Mike sent the two constables to search for him and asked me to explain what happened.

After listening carefully to our story, which Tim corroborated, he advised that both of us need to come to the police station to make a full statement as soon as they finished with the body.

While we were waiting, Mike examined the fire escape. He commented that it was safer to fall, then to try and climb down this fire escape. 'The owners of the building are in serious trouble as the fire escape is completely against all fire regulations and a danger to the occupants of the building.'

The two constables appeared with Mr Leonard Ndlovu, handcuffed him, and put him in the back of their patrol car.

Mike continued, grinning, 'This seems to be the end of the Mthetwa gang.'

'It certainly seems that way, although I never dreamed it would end this way. I hope there won't be any trouble resulting from this accident.'

Mike replied, 'I don't think you have anything to worry about, although they will hold an inquest. The coroner will decide. I think he will declare this as an accidental death. They will mention the owner of the building and report the bad state of the fire escape. They may bring Criminal charges against him.'

Tim and I followed Mike to the police station, where we made and signed our statements. Mr Ndlovu has also made his statement, blaming everything on Mr Mthetwa, even implicating him in the drug-dealing business.

I remarked to Mike, 'It would be nice if Mr Mthetwa's associates now also point the finger at him for Sarah's murder. That would clear my conscience, having brought her killer to justice.'

Tim asked Mike if we could have the files Mr Mthetwa took from the office. Mike disclosed that we would have to wait until after the inquest as they were evidence. He thought that they would hold the hearing within the next two weeks.

As it was late when we left the police station, I spent the night in my apartment. With the worry of Mr Mthetwa's gang now behind me, I decided to make this a permanent arrangement. Tomorrow I would give up my room at the Three Anchors pub.

I woke up the next morning feeling as if a significant load had been lifted from my shoulders, giving me the desire to face the future head-on. With Sarah's death avenged, life could now continue. I know she would be pleased.

I loved Sarah with all my heart. I don't know if I loved Jane, but Sarah is dead, and I must move on. Only by trying will I know if Jane and I are compatible. It is worth taking the chance, and I must.

At work that morning, I told Jane that I moved back to the apartment and asked, 'Would you mind redecorating the apartment for me as I am hoping that you will move in with me soon?'

Jane hugged me excitedly and replied, 'I thought you were never going to ask. Certainly, I will, immediately if you want. Can we re-furnish it as well?'

-The End-

Sidetracked

Printed in Poland
by Amazon Fulfillment
Poland Sp. z o.o., Wrocław